I'm the VILLAINESS, So I'm Taming the Final Boss

2

Sarasa Nagase

ILLUSTRATION BY
Mai Murasaki

YEN ON

New York

I'M THE VILLAINESS, SO I'M TAMING THE FINAL BOSS, Vol. 2
Sarasa Nagase

Translation by Taylor Engel
Cover art by Mai Murasaki

AKUYAKU REIJO NANODE LAST BOSS O KATTE MIMASHITA
©Sarasa Nagase 2018
First published in Japan in 2018 by KADOKAWA CORPORATION, Tokyo.
English translation rights arranged with KADOKAWA CORPORATION, Tokyo, through TUTTLE-MORI AGENCY, INC., Tokyo.

English translation © 2022 by Yen Press, LLC

Yen On
150 West 30th Street, 19th Floor
New York, NY 10001

Visit us at yenpress.com
facebook.com/yenpress
twitter.com/yenpress
yenpress.tumblr.com
instagram.com/yenpress

First Yen On Edition: February 2022

Yen On is an imprint of Yen Press, LLC.
The Yen On name and logo are trademarks of Yen Press, LLC.

Library of Congress Cataloging-in-Publication Data
Names: Nagase, Sarasa, author. | Murasaki, Mai, illustrator. | Engel, Taylor, translator.
Title: I'm the villainess, so I'm taming the final boss / Sarasa Nagase ;
    illustration by Mai Murasaki ; translation by Taylor Engel.
Other titles: Akuyaku reijou nanode last boss wo kattemimashita. English
Description: First Yen On edition. | New York, NY : Yen On, 2021
Identifiers: LCCN 2021030963 | ISBN 9781975334055 (v. 1 ; trade paperback) |
    ISBN 9781975334079 (v. 2 ; trade paperback)
Subjects: LCGFT: Fantasy fiction. | Light novels.
Classification: LCC PL873.5.A246 A7913 2021 | DDC 895.63/6—dc23
LC record available at https://lccn.loc.gov/2021030963

ISBNs: 978-1-9753-3407-9 (paperback)
        978-1-9753-3408-6 (ebook)

10 9 8 7 6 5 4 3 2 1

LSC-C

Printed in the United States of America

I'm the **VILLAINESS,** So I'm **Taming** the **Final Boss**

CONTENTS

Claude Jean Ellmeyer

Crown Prince of Imperial Ellmeyer.
The demon king and Aileen's fiancé.

James Charles

Misha Academy student council
president. The final boss of *Regalia
of Saints, Demons, and Maidens 2*.

Aileen Lauren
d'Autriche

A villainess who's remembered her past
life. However, her incomplete memories
are making it very hard for her to
avoid doom.

I'm the VILLAINESS, So I'm
Taming the Final Boss

Character Introductions
and Glossary

Walt Lizanis

Member of the Misha Academy
student council.
A fashion-conscious womanizer.

Auguste Zelm

Member of the Misha Academy
student council. A friendly,
skilled swordsman.

Kyle Elford

Member of the Misha Academy
student council. Quiet, serious,
and not much fun.

Rachel Danis

A student at Misha Academy.
The villainess of *Regalia of Saints,
Demons, and Maidens 2*.

The *otome* game *Regalia of Saints, Demons, and Maidens 2 ~ Kingdom's Fall and the Saint of Salvation*

When Lilia, the Maid of the Sacred Sword, killed the demon king, Imperial Ellmeyer was freed from the menace of the demons. Can our heroine, the unfortunate daughter of a count, find true love before she graduates? Meanwhile, having lost their king, the demons prepare their final act of resistance...

In the current world, the sacred sword has passed into Aileen's hands, meaning the story has already diverged from the one in the game.

When I was stripped of the sacred sword, the shock made memories of my past life come rushing back.

...If I said a thing like that, even if I am the protagonist, people would probably think I'd lost it. Or, in the world of this *otome* game, is there a chance they would accept it?

"All right. Good day to you, everyone."

Floating up into a storm of flower petals billowing through the clear sky, the demon king and his fiancée bid the assembly a refined farewell, then vanish. At that, finally, my fiancé seems to relax. He clicks his tongue in irritation. "Taking her leave in the middle of a ceremony! As always, that woman has no common sense. Are you all right, Lilia?"

"Huh? Oh, yes." I feign despondence, intentionally trying to act like my usual self.

My fiancé's eyebrows draw together, and he hangs his head. "...I'm sorry. If I wasn't so spineless, this never would have..."

"Don't say that, Cedric. It was my fault for angering Lady Aileen."

"It's not your fault," Marcus says supportively in agreement. He's standing behind me, wearing the uniform of the knightly order.

I feel the urge to burst out laughing, but I bite it back and shake my head, the way Lilia Reinoise would have done. *First things first: I have to make characters mine.*

I remember. I know now. The brilliant counselor-type who's a candidate to become the next prime minister. The coolheaded, mature one who's already made a success of himself in business. The cheerful yet surprisingly calculating future minister of foreign affairs. I know exactly what each character needs to hear to persuade them to become my allies. I should secure all the useful talent that's there for the taking.

Looking back, Lilia Reinoise's life had been a stormy one. Even so, there was never a time when there was no way forward. If she did her best, people acknowledged those efforts. If she talked things over with them, they understood. *You're a good girl*, they said, and accepted her.

All except for the demon king, Claude Jean Ellmeyer.

Or possibly the villainous Aileen Lauren d'Autriche.

As I tell the story of how I lost the sacred sword, I study the reactions of everyone around me. The people who sympathize clearly harbor more than a few doubts about the new crown prince.

There was a time when I didn't like this kind of maneuvering.

I'm done thinking that way.

I was so determined to help her, and it was all for nothing.

With the benefit of hindsight, I can see my old self in a more objective light, albeit only ever so slightly. What a child she was.

"Even if sad things happen, there are no bad people"? I mean, really!

I am the protagonist of this story.

"...Heh-heh. So she's supposed to be the main character, then?"

"Did you say something, Lilia?"

"Listen, Cedric. I'd like you to tell me something. Be honest."

This is the world of *Regalia of Saints, Demons, and Maidens*, an *otome* game. In my previous life, I'd lived in a different world known as Japan, an unbelievably developed place. That was where I played the game. Lilia no doubt remembers it.

Unfair high school days, where I watched classmates with worse grades than mine get babied and doted on. A family who only cared about appearances. Nothing went the way I wanted it to, and the only time I felt at peace was when I could be neck-deep in a game. I especially loved *otome* games that let you be a princess.

That life came to a sudden end in a car accident.

But who would've believed I'd be reborn in a game world? Hard to tell the difference between this and some game script.

There are loads of *otome* games to choose from. However, the *Regalia of Saints, Demons, and Maidens* series is the only one I've played dozens of times. And that's the one I've been reborn into? Seriously, how lucky can you get?

And now I'm certain. Everything up until the broken engagement event had followed the game's script. For some reason, though, Aileen Lauren d'Autriche didn't obsess over Cedric Jean Ellmeyer. Instead, she managed to get herself engaged to Claude, even though he should have been the one to kill her.

The villainess has romanced the final boss, the one character the heroine can't touch. It's far too convenient to be explained away as mere coincidence.

I have to know for certain whether she's like me.

Lilia's lips curve. She smiles at the fiancé she once thought she was in love with.

"Do you really love me, Cedric?"

"Lilia, don't you know the answer by now? Why ask such a thing?"

The first thing I need is time. Time and a plan that uses full knowledge of the game's story.

"—Are you sure you don't love Lady Aileen?"

Know what, villainess? I'm the one who's playing this game.

✦ First Act ✦
The Villainess Deceives Her Fiancé

A coach-and-four draws up in front of the gate known as the Saint's Triumphal Arch, and a lone figure in a navy-blue school uniform climbs out.

The arch marks the boundary of the town and the entrance to the academy. As traveling by coach on school grounds is prohibited, the carriage promptly pulls away. From beyond the gate, a young man in a similar uniform calls to the new arrival. "Uh... You Ailey Calois, the fellow who's transferring in?"

Looking up at the young man, she sees his hair is dark auburn, and he's the taller of them by several inches. Because she's tilted her head a bit, her short blond hair sways back and forth. So does the red tie that falls over her bound chest.

"Why yes— I mean, yeah, that's right. Who are you?"

"Ah, sorry to come out of nowhere like that. I'm Auguste Zelm, vice president of the Misha Academy student council. The president told me to bring you to the student council room, so I'm here to escort you. Um... Can I call you Ailey?"

She nods. It's close to her real name, which makes it easy to respond to.

"Thank you for your help, Mr. Zelm."

"Just call me Auguste. We're in the same year, you know. I'm not a fan of stuffy formalities." Auguste flashes her a friendly smile, telling her to follow him.

It's the noon recess. They enter the forecourt, which contains a fountain and several chatting students with their lunches spread on their laps. Several people steal glances at them, or more accurately, at Auguste. It's not hard to imagine how popular he is. Even now, he's walking slowly, matching Ailey's shorter stride. She's passing herself off as a boy, and he's still being considerate. No doubt he's kind to girls, as well.

As she's observing the people around them, he points toward a building and begins an impromptu explanation of the facilities. "That's the main school building. The east annex houses the faculty room as well as the principal's office, and the one on the west side is the student dormitory. If you draw lines between those three, they form a triangle. The structure in the center of that triangle is where the student council meets. There are other committee offices in there as well, so I guess you could say it's the home of the groups that run the school."

"I'd heard the rumors, but this place really is big. People often say students here have the right to self-government, and the student council is tremendously powerful." Judging from the fact that transfer students are taken to the student council room first instead of the faculty room, the rumors must be true.

"Yep. After all, the student council is often called 'Little Mirchetta' and 'the State in Miniature.' The teachers tend to avoid meddling in student affairs. In that sense, it's a good school—"

Screams and a ripple of murmurs interrupt Auguste's tour. At the same time, they start to hear angry shouts.

"I told you, I need sugar in my coffee!"

"I'm...I'm sorry!"

"You can't even manage a simple bit of shopping? Being engaged to someone like you is a rank embarrassment. On top of that, your family is mired in debt! What, is sugar too expensive for you?"

A male student is sneering at a girl. She hangs her head, pressing one hand to her struck cheek. Auguste clicks his tongue in irritation. "Him again...!"

"Cat got your tongue, you— Ow-ow-ow-ow! What gives?!"

She's twisted his arm up behind him, and the boy shrieks and looks back. She gives him a bright smile. "That's no way to treat a lady."

"Wh-what?"

"Then again, I guess you're actually still a child who can't have your coffee without sugar. Maybe that's why you don't have any manners?"

"You little runt—!"

The agitated boy's flailing is easy to evade. If she got injured over little things like this, her rivals would drag her down long before she became empress. Dodging a flying fist, she strikes him in the solar plexus. Even without much strength behind the blow, it's a precise attack, and the boy immediately crumples to his knees. She looks down at him, wiping off her fist with a handkerchief.

The boy groans, doubling over and hugging his stomach. "Who...are you...?"

"Me? I'm Ailey Calois. I just transferred in." She's smiling, but her eyes stay cold. "Apologize to her. Make sure you grovel."

"You wish! Who'd apologize to a girl?!"

"...I see. Yes, I had heard it was this sort of school."

Misha Academy is one of the finest educational institutions in the duchy of Mirchetta, a school where young men and women aged seventeen and older study side by side, regardless of differences in wealth or rank—that's the official line, at any rate. The reality differs quite a bit due to the duchy of Mirchetta's history as the birthplace of the Maid of the Sacred Sword, the saint who saved the nation.

When the Maid founded Imperial Ellmeyer, she left the region of Mirchetta to her parents. That's how the duchy was first established. As a result, for generations, the brothers of the Maid have served as dukes. Although the duchy is essentially a vassal state, as the homeland of the Maid's family, it possesses great autonomy within the empire.

However, a teaching left by the Maid of the Sacred Sword has warped the duchy's values. "Even shouldst thou have secured the world's salvation, ne'er forget thy duty as a woman." Said to have been handed down by the Maid herself, this teaching has produced a male chauvinist ideology, manifesting as a singular belief that women who haven't even saved the world have absolutely no right to defy men.

It was a convenient interpretation of the fact that, although the Maid had founded Imperial Ellmeyer, she had chosen to be empress rather than a ruling emperor. Most likely, the people in power at the time had feared the appearance of the Maid would improve women's social standing and upset the status quo.

That mindset is alive and well at Misha Academy, where many students aim to enter politics after graduation. The Maid of the Sacred Sword is considered holy, but despite that fact, women are not permitted to develop high opinions of themselves.

Well, as one who's known as the Maid of the Cursed Sword, that was never anything to do with me.

She snickers, taking care to keep her laughter as unfeminine as possible. "Unfortunately, I don't intend to follow the teachings of the Maid of the Sacred Sword."

"Wha...?"

"Men and women should support each other in equal measure. Granted, a child such as yourself who's helpless without the Maid may not be ready for that." Snubbing the stunned boy, she holds out a hand to the dazed girl. "Are you all right?"

"...Y-yes."

"I'd recommend breaking off your engagement to this piece of work. I'm sure it'll be life changing."

After giving the girl advice based on personal experience, she helps her to her feet. Then she helps brush the dust from her skirt and smooths her disheveled hair, putting everything back into place. As she works, she keeps an appropriate distance between them so she won't frighten the girl. She's also careful to be gentle—although, as an ordinary woman herself, she doesn't exactly have prodigious physical strength to begin with.

"Then if you'll excuse me, miss."

Leaving the blushing girl, she turns smartly on her heel. The students reflexively open up a path. When she looks up, in the distance, she can see the very top of the clock tower on the palace where the current duke of Mirchetta lives.

I will make you emperor.

To that end, she has to keep this country from collapsing.

Aileen Lauren d'Autriche's game isn't over yet, and at this point, what she has to do is—

"All right. Let my school life in drag begin!"

A male student who's been watching the commotion from a distance mutters to himself. "I told her to keep her head down! What's with the ladies' man act?"

"That was impossible for Lady Aileen from the very beginning, Master Isaac."

"…Well, this is all the demon king's fault to begin with."

Isaac is wearing the same uniform as Aileen, while Quartz and Luc are wearing white laboratory coats, disguised as research students. They gaze into the distance, resigned and philosophical. Isaac's shoulders slump dejectedly.

Two months previous—

"…Master Claude."

"What?"

"How many times must I ask you to refrain from this sort of thing while you are at work?! Unhand me, would you?!"

Aileen, who is arranging flowers in a vase in the office, scowls at the demon king who's wrapped his arms around her from behind. Despite her reprimand, his face stays buried in her shoulder and he doesn't move.

"I'm tired."

"Then I suggest retiring to your bedroom for a nap."

"I will if you'll come to bed with me," he whispers in her ear. She tries to slap him, but he easily catches her hand. Not only that, but the hand around her waist begins to move in suspicious ways, tracing the lines of her figure. Fending off that wandering hand, Aileen glares daggers at him.

"I believe you should go rest! By yourself! For a long time!"

"You're so cold. I'm merely asking my fiancée to comfort me."

"No, you're merely *teasing* me!"

"If you're referring to my request that we go to bed together,

I am quite serious and would greatly welcome it," he says with a straight face. She pinches the back of his hand, hard. Her crafty fiancé adopts a sorrowful tone. "I simply want to sleep with you in my arms."

"...H-holding me in your arms won't bring your work any closer to completion."

"I know. It's just that seeing you blush and panic soothes my heart."

"I am about to be very cross with you!"

"Good. I wouldn't be able to finish any of my work otherwise. I swear, unlike demons, humans are a demanding lot. They throw nothing but problems at me."

There's an unmistakable trace of fatigue in his voice, making it hard to be too upset with him.

Since regaining his position as crown prince, there's been no rest for Claude. He's begun making appearances at public functions, and he spends virtually every day buried in paperwork, fighting to stay on top of his battery of new duties. In particular, he seems to be in charge of mediating disputes between humans and demons. However, aside from Keith and Beelzebuth, he has few subordinates he can trust. In other words, he's shorthanded.

"Um... I could assist you, Master Claude."

Although she's made the offer many times before, his answer is always the same. "There's no need for that."

"I am your fiancée. It's only natural I support you."

"You're supporting me quite enough as it is." For just a moment, Claude's arms tighten around her, and then he lets go. He has to have noticed Aileen's dissatisfied expression, but he starts back to his seat and the work awaiting him.

Aileen presses her lips together, then takes up a position in front of his desk. "I have no intention of becoming an ornamental empress."

"I know."

"Then why won't you let me help you?"

"I'm the one the emperor is testing. He wants to know whether I will be capable of ruling both humans and demons." Claude raises his deep crimson eyes. "That means I am the one who should handle it. Have no fear: There are things only you can do. Meet me with a kiss whenever I return home, let me rest my head upon your lap—"

"As I said, that isn't what I meant!"

"—and try your best to stop avoiding such things just because you feel you're bad at them."

Chagrined, Aileen falls silent. Picking up his quill, Claude prepares to finally get back to work. "There's no need to worry. You're being a splendid fiancée."

He says it very matter-of-factly, and she blinks, then blushes. *That wasn't fair.*

Claude knows exactly why Aileen is anxious. Her desire to help Claude and be useful to him is genuine, of course. However, her desire has the shadow of a past failure behind it.

Once, Aileen had a fiancé who'd very publicly broken off their engagement. *I've fallen for another. I don't need you anymore.* At the time, she'd been busy trying to cope with several preposterous developments—memories of her previous life came rushing back just as she realized she was doomed to die if nothing changed—and she scarcely had the chance to fuss over something as trivial as the scar of a lost love.

Consequently, now that everything has more or less settled

down and she's gained another chance at romance, Aileen has little choice but to face her neglected wound.

Claude and her former fiancé, Cedric Jean Ellmeyer, are half brothers. It would be fair to say their contest for the throne occupies many of her thoughts. And the fact that Lilia Reinoise is Cedric's new fiancée can't be far behind, either.

"I'm only busy; I'm not in any particular trouble, and you have the Oberon Trading Firm to run. Relax and take life a bit easier."

"How could I, when you're working day and night?"

"That's precisely why you should. After all, any situation in which I have you help me is likely to be a bad one."

In other words, he isn't deliberately excluding her from his plans. All else aside, that's a relief.

She gazes at his perfectly gorgeous face. He's been working furiously, but he doesn't even have dark circles under his eyes. Granted, even if he did, this demon king would still be a work of art to look at. "Very well. What about selecting your outfits, then? I was hoping to find something that would be flattering when we made appearances together."

"Yes, that would be a great help. Ask Keith for the money."

"No, I'll pay. I'll mark it down as an Oberon Trading Firm expense— Oh, while we're at it, let's commission some formal attire for the demons as well. Since I've decided to take care of all of you, doing this much is simply part of my job." Aileen smiles brightly.

For the first time that day, Claude's face is marred by a complicated mix of emotions. "Let me just say that I am not, and have never been, your kept man."

"Have no fear. You are the only one who thinks so, Master Claude."

"You have that backward. You're the only one."

He may say that, but it's a fact that Aileen won over this man, the final boss of *Regalia of Saints, Demons, and Maidens.* She stands very straight, her expression composed. "All right. I'll get started right away, beginning with the demons."

"...Not with me?"

"They'll be far more challenging. You'd be beautiful even if all I did was drape some fabric over you."

"For someone who's trying to help me, you seem to be treating me very carelessly..."

"Demon king! Emergency! Emergency!"

An enormous bow tie–wearing crow flies out from behind Aileen. As she is Claude's fiancée, he shouldn't need to keep an eye on her at this point, but he hasn't made any attempt to remove the spell that allows demons to come and go through her shadow... That said, she has grown accustomed to it, and it's quite handy whenever she wants to summon a demon, so she has no plans to make him remove it, either.

"Gracious, Almond, what's the matter?"

"Humans! Lots of them! Right outside the forest!"

"Forest" means the forest ringing the once-abandoned castle where Claude and the demons live. Because Claude put a barrier around it, ordinary humans can't reach the castle. However, that hasn't stopped soldiers from surrounding the forest and threatening them before.

"Master Claude isn't simply the demon king. He's also the crown prince of this nation. What could possibly be the matter?"

"Rebellion, my king! Ashtart!"

"Milord, you're here, aren't you?!"

With a bang, the double doors of the office fly open. Keith

must have been running. He's still catching his breath as he starts speaking rapidly before Claude can say anything. "We just received a statement from a demon called Ashtart who claims to represent the demons of the Mirchetta region. Apparently he's gone against your orders and attacked a human village."

We refuse to acknowledge a demon king who's fallen to the Maid of the Sacred Sword.

Present the head of the Maid to us. If you do not, our next target will be Duke Mirchetta.

A missive to this effect had been delivered to the royal castle just as a small village in the duchy of Mirchetta was attacked.

Fortunately, most of the villagers were away doing migrant work for the summer, and the village had been nearly empty. The worst that had happened was that some children had fallen and gotten scrapes. At the end of the day, there had been no deaths. However, that didn't mean all was well.

Demons had attacked humans, against the demon king's will to boot. This naturally caused a huge commotion.

Part of the reason Claude had been allowed to reassume his position as crown prince was because humans had hoped it would give them control over the demons. That assumption had just encountered a very large and sudden hitch. Just when he needed to demonstrate his worth as crown prince, his worth as the demon king—which hadn't been a problem before—was now being called into question.

The faction that wanted to oust Claude and restore Cedric as the heir apparent certainly wouldn't let this incident slide without comment.

"Prepare emergency legislation regarding public aid in the event of demon attacks."

This is the first thing Claude says once they have all the available information. He looks at Isaac, who's been summoned to the office, then at Keith, and then finally at Aileen.

Quietly, Keith advises him, "If you do this now, they'll say you're trying to hide your blunder. Is that all right?"

"It doesn't matter. If I become emperor, everything to do with the demons will become the responsibility of the state. Aileen, please take this rough draft to Prime Minister d'Autriche. I can't push it through the court at my own discretion yet."

"Father won't pass a bill that does nothing but aid the demons."

Claude summarily puts Aileen's apprehension to rest. "The proposal also includes a provision guaranteeing demons will not let any harm come to humans." This from a man who'd never sent demons outside the barrier. Aileen gulps, then nods firmly.

Before, Claude had used the nonaggression pact to avoid getting involved with humans and their affairs. However, he can't only protect the demons if he's going to become emperor. Now that demons have actually attacked humans, unless he shows he's willing to use his authority over the demons to protect them, public support will undoubtedly wane.

"If we wait for the legislation to pass, aid won't reach the village today. It sounds as though there were a lot of children and elderly in that village; I'll have blankets, food, and other supplies sent through the Oberon Trading Firm... Isaac."

"I've already made the arrangements. Luc and Quartz brought out all the medicines they had in stock. Denis will head over there with a relief group and get to work on the rebuilding. The old geeze— Jasper is putting out a public call for additional relief supplies and fundraising. Oh, can we borrow some demons and employ them as Oberon staff members?"

"Of course. I don't mind."

Isaac whistles. "You've gotten flexible, Demon King."

"I already have Beelzebuth and Almond guarding the village."

"That's, uh…" Isaac hesitates, looking conflicted. He's probably concerned about possible friction with the villagers. Aileen wants to point that out as well, but she manages to hold back.

"Bel and Almond will be all right," Claude says reassuringly.

"…Yes, they will. I am the one who trained them, after all. And on the off chance they do fail, they'll most certainly be punished."

"Then that should do it for the moment—"

Cutting Isaac off, Claude speaks up again. "No, I wasn't finished. I've asked the emperor to make me the acting proxy for the duke of Mirchetta."

His remark startles Aileen considerably. Judging by his wry smile, Keith apparently saw it coming. "And then you'll capture Ashtart yourself, Master Claude? Well, that is the best way to get rid of this blot on your name."

"Do you really believe it will be so simple?! I even hear this commotion has caused the duke of Mirchetta to become bedridden, but…" Even as Aileen speaks, a different worry is growing in her mind. *Come to think of it, the duchy of Mirchetta… That's where Misha Academy is, isn't it? The stage for* Regalia of Saints, Demons, and Maidens 2. *Is this a coincidence?*

The *otome* game she'd played in her previous life, *Regalia of Saints, Demons and Maidens,* had centered around a slapdash background setting and a contrived storyline. For all that, though, the art and the voice acting were solid. The game had sold well and eventually expanded into a series. In other words, there was a sequel. They'd produced side stories and fan discs as well, and the series had been quite popular overall.

Aileen's memories of her past life are still vague, but she knows for a fact she'd played that second game. It had the thoroughly ominous subtitle *Kingdom's Fall and the Saint of Salvation*, and she remembers the general plotline. *Having lost their king, the demons descend upon the duchy of Mirchetta... I'm not sure I like where this is going.*

Although Claude is alive, the circumstances are eerily similar. Besides, if the demons destroy Mirchetta now, it will be a black mark on his reputation as crown prince, regardless of the reason. If nothing else, a future in which demons and humans live peacefully side by side will become a dim and distant possibility.

"Actually, Cedric was kind enough to give his approval. Only the formalities are left; all the groundwork has been laid."

"Master Cedric approved?"

If Cedric wants to retake the title of crown prince, his best move in this case is to watch and wait. However, instead of trying to exacerbate the chaotic situation, he's supporting Claude's efforts to bring it under control. Aileen can't help but find that extremely suspicious.

"In exchange for the duke of Mirchetta's safety, Ashtart asked for your head... You are Cedric's former fiancée. Maybe he's just worried about you," Claude says rather brusquely.

Aileen's eyebrows draw together in blatant disbelief. "That isn't even remotely possible."

"...Let's go with that, then. At any rate, if I am designated as the acting duke, I'll be able to deal with Ashtart whether he attacks or not. It's just a provisional measure until we capture him, so there isn't much opposition to the proposal. My request should go through. While I'm there, I can also make it perfectly clear that the demon king has no intention of making an enemy of the humans."

"Well, yeah, that's probably the best move... What sort of demon is this Ashtart, anyway?" Isaac asks.

Come to think of it, there had been no such demon in the game. *Does that mean this really is unrelated to the sequel...?* Making a snap decision at this juncture would be supremely risky, so Aileen decides to focus on listening very carefully instead.

"The demons of the Mirchetta region don't respond when I call them, and I have absolutely no information on Ashtart himself. It appears he can write, so I presume he has a humanoid form, like Bel. He's probably quite intelligent. The content of that statement was sound, and the demons of Mirchetta may be taking orders from him."

"As a rule, all demons should be head over heels for you, milord. Perhaps this means the intelligent ones have a unique capacity to rebel? ...Master Claude, after you capture this Ashtart, what should we do? Taking the wrong approach could make your path to the throne a great deal rougher."

"I'd prefer to respect the demons' autonomy. I don't intend to force any demon to obey me if they don't wish to."

"Master Claude." Because Claude was ostracized by human society, he treasures the demons. Aileen fully comprehends that. However, this is a completely different matter. Just as she's about to try convincing him, Claude's lips curve upward.

"—Of course, that only extends to autonomy within the bounds that I set."

When Aileen sees his diabolically beautiful face break into a cruel smile, she gulps. *This man is most certainly the demon king.*

Isaac seems to have picked up on that as well. He quickly averts his eyes, muttering, "In other words, you'll force his hand."

"I'll hear him out first. I've told them not to harm humans, and he has respected that, albeit just barely."

"Do you suppose that's why there weren't any deaths?" Keith wonders aloud.

"I think so. Either way, we'll have to find Ashtart first."

"Then I shall accompany you to Mirchetta, Master Claude." Due to the location, Aileen has to consider the potential connection to the game series. *If things start to follow the game's events, Mirchetta will fall. How could I just let that happen? Besides, I honestly can't convince myself that this is pure coincidence.*

For some reason, Aileen's thoughts turn to her former rival in love, the girl from whom she stole the sacred sword. In the sequel, Lilia Reinoise arrives to save the duchy of Mirchetta on the heroine's request, as the Maid of the Sacred Sword.

"No. You're the one they're after."

"I have the sacred sword. No demon can stand against me."

"And I expect Ashtart is well aware of that. In other words, he'll send humans after you."

"Would a demon be that cunning?!"

Aileen is genuinely surprised, and Keith bursts out laughing. Claude goes on impassively. "Some demons are more than a little crafty. You should stay in the capital. There's no guarantee that you wouldn't encounter human assailants in Mirchetta."

Keith picks up where Claude has left off. "Not only that, but that area's notorious for its fierce contempt of women. It might be unpleasant for you there."

"The d'Autriche name has more clout in the capital anyway. I'm with the demon king on this one."

"Isaac!"

"Fighting in unknown territory is a bad move. Plus you've got a ton of stuff to do here. You *are* the president of the enigmatic Oberon Trading Firm, after all."

"My thoughts exactly. For that very reason, I'd like to ask you to be my representative here while I'm away. All will be well. I'll return soon."

"You can teleport, Master Claude, so you say things like 'soon' quite casually, but...!" Aileen's the one being targeted, but she doesn't have to do anything? Unacceptable. *Besides, if the game's events really have begun, the church will be maneuvering on various fronts, and demon snuff will appear at Misha Academy!*

Demon snuff is a mysterious compound that lures demons with its scent and inhibits their rational thought. Many demons react violently to exposure and go on indiscriminate rampages. What's more, it has the same effect on humans. Those affected by the substance experience a moment of euphoria before flying into a rage, acting as if they've been dosed with an intense stimulant. A very troublesome element.

If someone were to use a thing like that on Claude...

It might be enough to turn him into the final boss again! No, even if he doesn't become a demon, it's also basically an aphrodisiac. If he ends up in that vulnerable state, with that face and that body...

Disaster. He could easily become "the demon king served by every woman in the world" or something along those lines. Aileen is determined to prevent that at all costs.

"Master Claude. I really can't leave that indecent face of yours alone."

"Indece... Where is this coming from?" Even when he looks

like he's fighting a headache, he's beautiful. It just isn't safe. Aileen throws her shoulders back and stands up straighter.

"I will go as well."

"Absolutely not. It's too dangerous."

"I promise you I'll be useful!"

"If you truly want to help me, then stay here and behave, please." Putting it like that isn't fair. Aileen bites her lip. Claude speaks with the same firmness he uses whenever he tells her he doesn't need help. "I won't take you with me. I will become emperor, and you will be empress. Are you saying you can't respect my decision?"

"...No..."

Aileen realizes it's pointless. At the moment, she doesn't have enough information to convince Claude.

Would he believe her if she revealed everything and told him about the game? Even if he did, she doesn't actually know exactly what's happening, either. She probably can't explain it to anyone's satisfaction.

However, what if the current troublemakers—Ashtart and the demons of Mirchetta—are under the influence of demon snuff? And what if the one manipulating them is the same final boss as in the game?

Yes, the sequel had a final boss as well. One who'd used demon snuff to compel the demons to assault and destroy Mirchetta—

"I'll take Keith with me. We'll leave tomorrow. Keith, get ready."

"Understood, milord."

"Will you be teleporting yourselves there, then?" Aileen asks.

"Yes. The sooner we arrive, the better."

As of right now, the scenarios that surface in Aileen's mind are nothing more than theories. However, if they misread the situation, the resulting wound will almost certainly be fatal. Aileen draws a deep breath. "Very well."

"...You're convinced already? Really?"

She smiles at her fiancé. His instincts are quite sharp. "Yes. You can teleport, Master Claude, and it keeps you from understanding how women feel."

Claude's eyebrows draw together. Keith blinks. Isaac says "Hey...," but she raises her voice, deliberately talking over him. "You assume we can meet whenever we please. You don't know how I feel when I'm left behind."

"I don't think that's the case..."

"Master Claude. I asked you to let me accompany you, but you refused. I will ensure that you feel the full weight of that refusal."

Claude looks wary. Aileen gives him her very best smile. "While you are the proxy of the duke of Mirchetta, I forbid you from using teleportation to come and see me. Let us pursue an ordinary, human sense of distance."

"...Is this your idea of revenge?"

"It is a trial for lovers who must spend time apart. If you do not abide by it, I will consider it grounds for breaking off our engagement."

There's a short pause, and then sudden lightning flashes in the evening sky.

The demon king's emotions affect his surroundings in the form of abnormal weather. However, even if a whirlwind springs up or the earth splits open, Aileen has absolutely no intention of giving in.

★　　★　　★

Evidently, Aileen's current fiancé loves her quite deeply. Claude agonizes over his decision for a while, but even then, he just can't agree to take Aileen along. After checking several times to confirm it was acceptable to send letters delivered by demons, he departs.

Aileen sees him off with a smile. Then she promptly sets to work.

She is, of course, preparing to infiltrate Misha Academy, the stage of *Regalia of Saints, Demons, and Maidens 2*.

If the game's events are already in progress, it's very likely that the duchy of Mirchetta will fall before Ashtart becomes relevant. The potential presence of demon snuff is problematic as well. She decides it will be best to dispose of it quietly. With her knowledge of the game, she's the only one who can anticipate all the impending trouble and deal with it in advance.

Claude won't reverse his decision because of mere emotion. Aileen hinted at broken engagements, and even then, he ultimately left her behind on principle. That's the sort of person he is. Unless she finds persuasive proof of some sort, he's certain to forcibly send her back the moment he discovers her.

In other words, Aileen has to search Misha Academy and—if the game events really have been set in motion—alter the course of events so that the duchy of Mirchetta can avert disaster, all without letting Claude discover her clandestine presence.

On top of that, Misha Academy is situated in the same town as the duke's residence where Claude will be living. The estate is so close to the school grounds that you can actually spot it from the top of any tall building on campus.

If the game hasn't started, I'll leave immediately. If we run into each other on the street, it will be a total fiasco!

However, since Aileen is the one with knowledge of the game, it's vital she infiltrates the academy in person. To that end, she makes preparations to do so without alerting Claude.

Her collaborators are the Oberon Trading Firm executives: Isaac, Denis, Luc, Quartz, and Jasper, a journalist. She also drags Almond and the other demons into the affair by telling them there are reports coming from Misha Academy of a certain type of incense that's hazardous to demons, and she wants to help Master Claude. Naturally, they press her for explanations, but she can't tell them about the game. Instead, she bulls her way through with the assertion that she needs to go in order to confirm her suspicions.

None of the others can be as high-handed with her as Claude, and in the end, they seem to decide they can't let her act on her own. Reluctantly, they agree to go along with her—on the condition that, as Isaac puts it, "If the demon king finds out, this is all on you!"

They decide that Luc and Quartz will infiltrate Misha Academy's graduate school as research students, while Isaac will accompany Aileen as a fellow student.

This is just to be on the safe side. The moment it's clear that this has nothing to do with the game, we'll leave at once! If Claude suspects her, he'll send her back before she can blink. To that end, everyone in the group assumes false identities, keeping nothing but their names. Aileen's father, Duke d'Autriche, loves seeing his daughter get herself into sticky situations, which meant they had his cooperation. Consequently, their documents are flawless. They stagger their entry times and vary their reasons for entering the academy, while Aileen falsifies her name and even her gender, just in case.

The result is the fun school life in drag she's just commenced.

"I'm so glad I had Mother teach me how to pass myself off as a man..."

"Did you say something, Ailey?"

"No, nothing important." Aileen smiles back at Auguste. He doesn't seem suspicious of her. He probably thinks she's just a rather small-boned boy.

I've cleared the first hurdle, then. If Auguste is at the academy, though, does it mean the game really has begun?

Auguste Zelm was a full-fledged love interest in the game.

After Lilia, the Maid of the Sacred Sword, slew the demon king, Imperial Ellmeyer had been liberated from the menace of the demons. *Regalia of Saints, Demons, and Maidens 2 ~ Kingdom's Fall and the Saint of Salvation* begins immediately after that. Can the heroine, the unfortunate daughter of a count, find true love before graduation? Meanwhile, having lost their king, the demons commence their final act of resistance—that's the gist of the sequel. In the story, Auguste was the main hero. During the best ending, he borrowed the sacred sword from Lilia, killed the final boss, and won the title of Holy Knight.

"Still, you're tough. The boy who was harassing that student was built much bigger than you are."

"I dabble in self-defense. You're quite tall yourself, Auguste, and you look strong."

"I'm confident in my sword skills, but I've still got a long way to go. I'm sorry about that business earlier, though. There's been quite a lot of that here lately. If we had more men like you, I think this school would change, but...," he murmurs. He's an upright hero, and the deep-seated contempt for women at this academy disgusts him. He feels women should be protected. It's a result of the guilt he has over being unable to protect his mother—or so his backstory says, but Aileen decides that doesn't matter right now. She hasn't gone to the trouble of infiltrating this place disguised as a boy to romance the characters.

That said, the heroine, the final boss, and the major love interests are all members of the student council, so I do want more information on it. Getting close to him would be an intelligent move. In order to improve our relationship score, I need to say... Wait, but he thinks I'm a boy. Will it still work?

"Here's the student council room."

She refocuses her attention on the door directly in front of her. Auguste slowly pushes it open, revealing the figure inside.

"What's going on, Auguste?" the student says mildly. His uniform looks particularly good on him, and the year badge gleaming on his collar tells her that he's one grade ahead of them.

"Oh, Walt. This is rare. You're never in the student council room—don't tell me... You're not hiding from another girl again, are you?"

"Don't say it like that. You make it sound as if I'm constantly getting chased by girls."

As she watches the two of them chat, Aileen delves into her game knowledge. Walt Lizanis, the student council's Casanova treasurer. He's another love interest. He's kind to women, which makes him popular, but that's only the face he shows to the world. He's a rather precocious character, hiding secrets behind his smile.

Oh, honestly! It's exactly like the game! I can't be certain until I meet the heroine, but from the look of it, the game does seem to be underway.

"It's just you, Walt? Where's Kyle?"

"In the library. He said he wanted to eat somewhere quiet."

Kyle was another treasurer. Naturally, he was also a love

interest. The game portrayed him as a serious character, in contrast to Walt. Both he and Walt played major roles in the fight against the demons.

Well, that aside— The heroine isn't here, is she?

The heroine is Serena Gilbert. She's seventeen, in the same year as Auguste. If the game's story holds true, she will have joined the student council as its secretary because he asked her to.

If she isn't here, the game's events shouldn't start. Aileen holds on to a flicker of hope, but Walt unintentionally provides her with her answer. "By the way, Auguste, Serena left the minutes from the meeting the other day. She wants you to look them over. They're on that desk."

Oh, so she is here. Nearly resigned at this point, Aileen listens intently to their conversation.

"All right. It's impressive that she finished this fast. What a hard worker."

"A hard worker, hmm...? Well, if she wants to become Princess Lily White, she'll have to be that. And who might this be?"

Walt gives Aileen an appraising glance, so she bows politely. "It's good to meet you. I'm Ailey Calois, a transfer student."

"Hmm. You're awfully cute... Well? What does a transfer student need with the student council?"

"James sent me to fetch him— Huh? Actually, where is James?"

"Back in the reference room, looking up the procedures used for past school festivals. The president's the real hard worker around here."

"Oh... Sorry, Ailey, hang on just a minute. I'll go grab him."

Auguste heads for the door at the back of the room. In between his calls of "James," Walt stands up and comes over to her. "The president is scary, so I'll excuse myself, transfer student. Good luck."

"Thanks." Aileen assumes he's going to walk past her, but he stops instead. She looks up, wondering what's wrong. Walt has bent down so that his face is right in front of hers. Aileen Lauren d'Autriche would have slapped him on reflex, but he's caught her off guard so completely that she freezes up instead.

"...You smell good."

"Um, what?"

"I'm sensitive to smells. You know how they say pretty girls smell nice?"

Maybe because he surprised her earlier, Aileen manages to respond without seeming flustered. "If you say so. I haven't had a sweetheart yet myself. By the way, Walt, you're getting awfully close."

If Claude heard her say she didn't have a lover, it would probably start to rain. The thought is oddly calming. In response to her cool remark, Walt apologizes and steps back. "When you do find a sweetheart, by all means, see for yourself. I'll catch you later, then."

Since Walt is a year ahead of her, she thinks they're very unlikely to run into each other again. As he leaves, though, his meaningful smile never flickers. *I don't think he's caught on to the fact that I'm a girl, but...it's not as if I'm wearing perfume...*

Concerned, she sniffs at the hem of her uniform, but the only thing she smells is the clean scent of soap. Just as she's starting to worry that smelling like soap might not be manly, Auguste emerges from the room in back. "You're the one who summoned him. Get a grip."

"Just have him wait. I'm busy."

A figure emerges, brushing dust off his clothes. His back is to the light, and she can't make him out well. Aileen narrows her eyes, waiting for the boy to take up his position in front of the president's desk.

His name is James Charles. By rights, he should have been a young noble of Mirchetta—and when she's remembered that much, she has to bite back a wry smile. His background really does resemble Claude's.

This is the character who becomes the final boss in Game 2. He's the president of Misha Academy's student council, which holds vast power in the school—typical for an *otome* game. In contrast to Auguste, he has pale hair and eyes like clear glass beads. He possesses an inhuman beauty...which is only natural. As exemplified by the demon king, demons are beautiful without exception. Since he's half demon, it makes perfect sense that James is also very attractive.

That's right: the final boss of Game 2 suffers from the fact that he's a cambion.

Due to his unusual parentage, the duchy of Mirchetta wants him dead. Neither fully demon nor fully human, there's no place for him in either group. In the game, as he's driven farther and farther into a corner, he uses demon snuff, incites the demons to war, and lashes out at Mirchetta as a whole. Then he discards his humanity, declares himself the demon king's successor, searches for a place to belong, and is finally laid low by the sacred sword.

He may not have done anything yet, though.

She'll have to look into this carefully. After all, she is the woman who's going to marry the demon king. If James hasn't done anything, passing judgment on him just because he's half demon would make her a failure as the demon king's wife. She won't dispose of him out of hand just to keep the game from progressing.

"So you're Ailey Calois, the transfer student? Auguste told me about you. Starting trouble as soon as you arrive... What a headache."

"James. I already told you the other party was to blame. That isn't what I was trying to say."

"If you're going to cause problems every time someone so much as hits a girl, I'll have you leave at once."

"—'So much as hits a girl'?"

Auguste has been standing his ground with James, but at Aileen's low voice, he freezes up. However, James takes a seat in the president's chair, pretending not to notice. Anyone would think he was some sort of sovereign.

"That kind of thing is very common. If we made a commotion out of every single incident, there'd be no end to it."

"In other words, the student council president has no intention of improving the situation here?"

He gives her a scornful smile. "That's the trouble with transfer students: You always get the wrong idea. If you want to pretend to be a defender of justice, earn yourself status that allows you to speak. Also, in this academy, my word is absolute. Remember that."

Right. Come to think of it, he was this sort of character. Once she's remembered that, Aileen's well-trained facial muscles keep her smile firmly in place. It looks as though she'll be able to obey Isaac's orders not to stand out.

"That's all I had to say. I'm busy with preparations for the school festival. You may return to the dormitory and look forward to tomorrow and the rest of your days here at school… After all, I'm sure nothing good will actually come of them."

James heads back into the reference room. Still smiling, Aileen thinks *Master Claude really is amazing.* He is strong, but he doesn't let his strength go to his head. She feels as if she might succumb to that temptation; she still has a long way to go. As his fiancée, she'd like to improve herself.

That being the case, she refrains from striking at the cambion's back with the sacred sword.

The next day, as she gazes at her shredded math textbook, Aileen remembers something nostalgic. *I had this done to me when I was Master Cedric's fiancée as well. I suppose neither gender has a monopoly on bullying.*

The seats in the classroom are arranged in the shape of a spiral. Some of the boys in those seats are smirking, and she recognizes one of the faces in that group. It's the boy Aileen publicly humiliated yesterday. What an obvious stunt.

Neither Auguste nor Isaac is in her class. This is her first day attending lectures, and she has no acquaintances here, let alone friends. Students who have nothing to do with the matter keep darting glances at her.

Well now, what should I do? she thinks. Just then, a timid figure approaches her.

"Um…"

"You're, uh…the girl from yesterday…"

"Y-yes. My name is Rachel Danis."

"Rachel Danis?!" Aileen echoes, more loudly than she means

to. Rachel flinches, and she hastily makes excuses. "I-I'm sorry. You have exactly the same name as a girl I know, and it surprised me."

"I—I suppose it would." Rachel still looks perplexed, but she nods, making her soft hair sway back and forth. She has the shy gaze of a small animal, and Aileen feels rather apologetic—and surprised.

Rachel Danis is the villainess of Game 2.

Had her character always been this fragile and pretty? She starts to wonder, then thinks better of it. Rachel is a schemer who only pretends to be fragile in front of the boys.

Unlike Aileen, the villainess in the previous game, Rachel Danis's looks and noble rank were only a little above average. This made her a bit drab for a villainess, but she made up for her other shortcomings with cunning. She clung to the heroine like a remora, and yet, out of deep feelings of inferiority over her own apparent mediocrity, she spread spiteful rumors in secret and stole the attentions of the love interests for herself.

In that case, could this kindness be merely an act…?

But she'd been shocked by the sight of that male student hitting her, and she just can't bring herself to think of it that way.

"Um… The Academic Affairs Department loans textbooks to students who've forgotten theirs, so…"

"Hey! Rachel! What are you doing? Get over here!" the boy from yesterday yells. The girl ducks her head. That doesn't seem like an act, either. Aileen saved her yesterday, so although she knows her fiancé will be angry, this girl still mustered up the courage to come over and give her a word of advice. That's all it looks like.

…She's a good girl. Besides, even in the game, I felt rather sorry for her.

During the school festival event, she'd ended up competing against the heroine. Driven by her desire to win, Rachel had resorted to all sorts of petty schemes but had been exposed and condemned for them. Her line at that point—"I wanted to be someone special, too"—struck a chord in many players.

Besides, Aileen wants to believe her own instincts over the game's scenario. She smiles at Rachel. "You don't have to worry about it. It isn't your fault."

Rachel's eyes widen. As she watches, Aileen scrapes together the fragments of what used to be her textbook, then dumps them into the garbage where they belong. Then, speaking loudly enough that both Rachel and the boys beyond her can hear, she says, "I'm not so incompetent that I'd be in trouble without a textbook."

When she was engaged to the crown prince, this sort of thing happened all the time. Since she insisted on paying her opponent back in kind until they gave up, there were times people treated her as if she was the aggressor, even though she'd been the victim all along. However, if the alternative is making Rachel anxious, she doesn't mind if that happens here as well.

Seating isn't assigned in the lecture hall, so she settles herself right in front of the platform, where there are bound to be fewer students. Immediately afterward, the teacher enters and class begins.

All right. What would be the most effective next move?

Before the Maid of the Sacred Sword appeared, the Mirchetta region had seen fierce fighting with the demons. Demon snuff was an accidental by-product of that struggle. While it attracted demons and made them more dangerous, for humans who developed a tolerance for it, it boosted their physical abilities. In other words, it made it possible to create enhanced humans. As a result, in the past, Mirchetta had given its soldiers demon snuff before dispatching them to fight demons.

However, the stuff was highly addictive, and it kept ruining people. The Church of Mirchetta—which would later venerate the Maid of the Sacred Sword and become the empire's largest religion—eventually assumed control of its use and distribution. The very existence of demon snuff was covered up. Not only that, but an ingredient called "opym" was needed in order to refine it, and information had been so tightly controlled hardly anyone alive remembered what opym was anymore. At present, demon snuff simply wasn't normally made.

That said, the game had described opym. It was made from a plant that had bright red flowers and yielded fruit the size of chicken eggs. In order to make opym, one cut slits in that fruit, dried the milky liquid that oozed from it, then turned what they harvested into a powder... In other words, the game had depicted opium as opym. What was needed in order to make opym— and demon snuff—were opium poppies. The game developers had probably intended to give the substance a forbidden aura by making one of its key ingredients a plant whose cultivation was banned in Japan.

Parenthetically, in this world, neither opium poppies nor opium itself are forbidden. As a matter of fact, they are one of the crops grown on the farms Cedric took from Aileen.

She'd charged Quartz and Luc with locating and confiscating the wild poppies growing on school grounds. They intentionally left a few so they could see who, if anyone, tried to harvest them. *For the moment, I've dealt with the demon snuff. Now I just have to get the duchy of Mirchetta onto a route where it won't be destroyed!*

Just as Claude had laid waste to Imperial Ellmeyer in most

scenarios, James ended up destroying the duchy of Mirchetta in many of the Game 2 routes. The one route on which it was possible to stop the final boss was Auguste's path, wherein Auguste borrowed the sacred sword and killed James.

However, as the woman who will become the demon king's wife, that route is essentially unavailable to Aileen.

At any rate, the game does seem to have started. First, I'll need to meet with Serena, the heroine, and find out how far it's progressed.

"—lois. Ailey Calois!"

She isn't used to hearing her false name yet, and it takes her a moment to register it. The teacher has called on her. "Yes." Aileen stands up.

The disagreeable-looking mathematics teacher is holding a piece of chalk. "Transfer student. You caused a disturbance on your first day, and now you're attending class without a textbook. You seem very cavalier about all this. You must be brilliant—what's the answer to the problem on page 137?"

"Three, sir," Aileen responds immediately, then resumes her seat.

The teacher's eyes go very wide. She can tell he was trying to make an example of her for not having her textbook open instead of just giving her a warning, as would have been appropriate. A nasty way of doing things. Confirming her suspicions, the teacher's tone is bitter. "…Correct."

Ooooh. A subdued stir spreads through the room.

"You're a very lucky boy." The teacher spits out the words quietly. Apparently he doesn't plan to take another shot at her, though, and class resumes.

The trick is a simple one: In the game, the heroine had been called on to answer the same problem during class. Aileen had simply remembered the answer.

Still, to think that just because of yesterday's incident, even the teachers have their eyes on her now. At this rate, it may be hard to get close to Serena without standing out while she's disguised as a boy. It isn't as if just greeting her once will be enough. Aileen will have to stay in regular contact with her. She'll need a good reason.

Serena's the student council secretary, so if I join the council... Isaac will be angry, won't he?

However, the situation clearly demands a little recklessness. By the time Aileen's worked out her plan to a certain extent, the bell rings, signaling the end of morning classes.

With her textbook gone, Aileen is traveling light. She leaves the classroom to go to the one next door, looking for Auguste. She's managed to get acquainted with him rather neatly, so there's no point in not taking advantage of it.

At the sight of the two figures in the corridor, though, she stops.

Serena Gilbert!

"...You want me to give this letter to Auguste?"

The sunlight shines through the girl's perfectly straight silver hair, giving it a glow. Her flawless posture, the outline of her clear, even-featured face, her eyebrows set in a determined expression— unlike Lilia, the heroine of the previous game, she's depicted as a practical girl who's rather credulous, but good at looking after others. She's even supposed to be a skilled cook.

However, her family circumstances are complicated.

While she is the legitimate daughter of Count Gilbert, her parents died when she was very young, and her uncle's family yanked the title out from under her. Now that the uncle has frittered away her inheritance, he decided to marry her off to a wealthy nouveau riche man more than twenty-five years her senior as soon as she graduates from Misha Academy in exchange for securing a loan. In other words, her days at this school are the last time she'll ever be free.

Just before entering the academy, during the game's opening, she had written a letter to someone she idolized. *"I just know I'll change my fate, the way you did,"* she'd said.

Girls and boys aged seventeen and older were allowed to enroll at Misha Academy and attend for two years. If they continued their studies at the graduate institute, it could take up to three years for them to finish. Meanwhile, the school was very strict when it came to letting students advance to the next year. Instead of being held back, students with poor grades were simply expelled. This was true in the game as well. The graduation date changed depending on Serena's parameters and how far her romance had developed. At the same time, her romantic progress affected how much time remained before the duchy of Mirchetta would be destroyed.

In other words, at a minimum, the game could end after one year.

If Ashtart has some connection to the game... I wonder if we aren't rushing headlong toward the bad ending: total destruction within the first year.

Aileen decides to stay where she is and observe Serena. It's the noon recess, and there are other students in the hall; if she keeps a little distance between them, she won't be noticed.

"Yes, I'd like you to give it to Master Auguste for me. I heard you would help with requests like that, Lady Serena... Everyone was saying they'd expect no less from Princess Lily White." The other girl looks down, embarrassed.

Serena seems a little troubled. "But aren't you already seeing someone? Will this be all right?"

"I—it's fine! A little while ago...when I, um...made my lover angry, Master Auguste stepped in and stopped him. I want to thank him for that in some small way."

Slowly, Serena accepts the letter. She nods, smiling. "All right. Leave it to me. I'm not Princess Lily White yet, though."

"Wh-what are you saying? There's no one it could be this year but you, Lady Serena! You're lovely, your grades are good, you're reliable, and you don't put on airs just because you're a count's daughter!"

"Thank you. But I'm rather lacking in etiquette..."

"I-I think you will be chosen as Princess Lily White, Lady Serena. You stand up for girls. If someone like you wins the title, I don't think girls will be forced into relationships with boys they don't even like, the way I was..."

The girl looks down, smiling through her tears. As she gazes at the striking scene, Aileen frowns. *In the game, I never realized girls were being treated quite this poorly.*

Princess Lily White was a girl chosen at the school festival for being the greatest lady at the academy, and there was an unwritten rule that even the male students had to respect her. Depending on her parameters, Serena could become that girl. On top of that, although initial opinions of her had been *She's just a girl, how dare she?* they changed to *She's a girl, so how did she manage that?* as her romance progressed. This meant the difference was rather subtle.

"Are you in some sort of trouble?"

"...I—I mean, I know a nobody like me should be terribly grateful for an offer like this, but...wh-when he told me there was no knowing what the other boys would do to me if I refused, I was frightened..."

"Then would you like me to broach the subject of breaking up in your place?"

"What...? W-would you really?" The girl's expression is a mixture of surprise and delight.

Serena nods firmly. "I'll speak to him. Leave it to me."

"Th-thank you so much!"

Aileen listens to their exchange, arms folded... *Well, perhaps? If she goes about it the wrong way, it's going to be catastrophic, but... Since she's the protagonist and all, it might go well.*

"You'll have to get a little stronger, though, so that you'll be able to speak for yourself."

"Y...yes. I'm sorry."

"Lady Lilia, the Maid of the Sacred Sword, has continued to support Prince Cedric Jean Ellmeyer even though he's been deprived of his rightful position as crown prince. You mustn't let a few hardships discourage you."

Oh, there it is. I knew it. Aileen raises her eyes to the ceiling.

Lilia Reinoise had risen from a common background to the station of duke's daughter, become engaged to the man she loved, and had even proved to be the Maid of the Sacred Sword. A girl her own age who had changed fate—that was Serena's idol, the person who gave her hope.

Since Lilia isn't the Maid of the Sacred Sword anymore, there is a chance that might have changed, but...it hasn't, has it?

Strangely, that simple discovery has worn Aileen right out. Just then, someone thumps her lightly on the shoulder, and she nearly jumps out of her skin.

"Hey, Ailey."

"A-Auguste!"

"Oh, sorry. Did I startle you?" Auguste gives a little laugh.

It's contagious; Aileen laughs, too, one hand pressed to her bound chest. "You sure did. Need something?"

"Mm... Well, remember the girl you saved yesterday? She looked as if she wanted to tell me something. Then I heard a rumor that your textbook had been torn up, so I thought you might be feeling a bit down..." Auguste scratches his cheek in mild embarrassment. Apparently, he's been worried about her.

"I'm fine. Who needs textbooks, anyway?"

"You know, you're short, but you're really cool. Don't do anything reckless, though. If you ever need someone to talk to, I'm always—"

"Auguste!" Before he's finished that thought, a loud voice drowns him out. Serena comes trotting down the corridor, her cheeks flushed. Aileen didn't expect the person she is after to come to her, and it takes a moment to register.

"Say, do you suppose we could go home together after school today? I'd like to get your advice on a certain matter. A moment ago, a girl came to me for help. It's been happening a lot lately... But when they tell me they're in trouble, I just can't seem to turn them away. You're concerned about it as well, aren't you, Auguste?"

Aileen frowns. What Serena is saying doesn't quite mesh with what Aileen overheard.

"If she's in trouble, sure, that's concerning... But where is she?"

"I'll mediate, so that doesn't matter. Can we make it just the two of us?"

"You mean you can't tell me about it right here, right now?"

"Certainly not! It's a delicate matter, so we'll need to be alone. Possibly in a café somewhere."

And yet she's saying all of this right in front of Aileen, or rather, Ailey. Auguste might be thinking something similar; he offers a vague smile. "Hmm... But the school festival's coming up, and things are busy. Why don't we talk in the student council room instead? If we go to a café together on our own after school and people get the wrong idea, it'll make things awkward for both of us."

When she hears that, Aileen stiffens up. *They still aren't close enough to go home from school together?! That can't be good!* It's the autumn term already. If the game is going to end in a year, they're already more than halfway through. *Then again, if the affection level is currently rated as friendship, whether or not there's a chance to go home from school together is determined at random.* As Aileen is doggedly trying to hang on to hope, Serena suddenly looks over at her.

"Auguste, who is this?"

"Oh, he's Ailey. You know, the student who transferred in yesterday."

"You are? ...The one who said he wouldn't obey the Maid of the Sacred Sword?"

It isn't her imagination—Serena's tone has suddenly gone cold.

"Auguste. You're welcome to get along with everyone, but you should choose your friends carefully. It's outrageous that any-one would speak ill of Lady Lilia. Do you intend to align yourself with the demons, Auguste?"

"Huh... N-no, Ailey saved a girl, and then—"

"Rachel, wasn't it? She's been sneaking out to meet someone at night. That's why her fiancé is angry with her. I find it quite boorish to interfere in the private quarrel of a betrothed couple. You mustn't get involved, Auguste."

Serena has just agreed to do that very thing, but perhaps it hasn't occurred to her just yet. Rudely, she looks Aileen over from head to toe, then shrugs. "All right, I'm going to lunch. I'll bring refreshments to the student council again later. Do look forward to it." With a wave and a smile for Auguste, Serena walks away.

Aileen stays where she is, looking dazed. Auguste turns to her apologetically. "I'm sorry, Ailey. Serena's a decent sort, but she idolizes the Maid of the Sacred Sword like you wouldn't believe."

"The Maid... You mean Lady Lilia? But she isn't the Maid anymore."

"Don't say that in front of Serena. She'll be furious and start on her rant about how Aileen Lauren d'Autriche is evil without precedent, how she's the lackey of demons, and how she should return Lady Lilia's sword to her... She's been particularly fero-cious about it lately."

Evil without precedent, hmm? How marvelous. Aileen very nearly smiles like a villainess.

"Ailey, are you angry? I'm sorry, I just..."

"No, I've made up my mind. I'd like to ask you for a favor, Auguste."

"Keep your head down," Isaac told her, over and over, mak-ing his cooperation contingent on her keeping her word. Aileen decides right then and there to go back on her promise with a smile.

She found the love interests and the heroine all in place at the school. That means the game's events have most definitely been set into motion. She doesn't know who Ashtart is and how he fits into all this, but if the game is in progress, James will destroy

Mirchetta someday. In that case, Aileen can help Claude by preventing that disaster from ever coming to pass.

I'll show them the power of a woman whose evil has no precedent.

All else aside, she's the one who managed to romance the final boss.

She's sure she'll be able to keep the final boss of Game 2 from manifesting as well. Like Claude, she'll just have to tame James. For Claude's sake.

"I'd like you to help me join the student council. In order to protect the girls of this academy, you see."

Claude signs his name at the end of the letter, then folds it carefully.

When Aileen told him she'd consider breaking off their engagement, he'd started thinking of ways to retaliate. Still, it's actually rather nice to exchange letters like this and stay mindful of "normal human distance." He mustn't lose the ability to present himself as a normal human. Not if he's going to rule over humans as well.

"Master Claude. Members of a parent group known as the Ladies of the White Lily are waiting in the drawing room. It's about the Misha Academy incident."

"Yes, I'm on my way... Keith." After he's sealed the letter, Claude asks for advice on a matter that's been troubling him. "Do you suppose she'd be angry if I teleported the letter into her hands?"

"I think it would be safer not to. Human lovers do have to wait for letters, after all."

"I see... In that case, have Almond deliver this one."

With an exaggerated bow, Keith slips the letter into his jacket. "Milord, do your job instead of simply obsessing over your beloved. Duke Mirchetta's lazy son has it in for you, you know. You fired everyone he had influence over."

"By sheer coincidence, that's how it turned out when I got rid of all the incompetents. If he's so proud of being related to the Maid of the Sacred Sword, he should use his abilities to vanquish the demon king." With a thin smile, Claude rises to his feet and heads out of the room, his cloak flaring.

Since he's doing his best not to use magic in public, he walks to the drawing room. Keith rolls his eyes, then follows him. "By the way, that lazy son is funneling quite a lot of money to the church. He's apparently asked them to assassinate his nephew."

"Nephew? Duke Mirchetta only has two children, and he said his daughter died quite some time ago. Did she have an illegitimate child?"

"Something like that, yes. The duke himself is completely unaware; his good-for-nothing son is hiding it from him. From what I hear, the girl eloped nearly twenty years ago. With a demon."

Claude stops in his tracks. "...Then you're telling me there's a cambion?" he asks quietly.

"That's right. And the lazy son fears this child. And though the duke was apparently furious when he heard his daughter had eloped with a demon, he'd doted a great deal on her. On the other hand, he and his son have never gotten along. If the duke knew his daughter had a child, the son suspects he might choose his nephew to succeed him instead."

"Even if that nephew is half demon?"

"A cambion could pass as a human. That's another reason why the unworthy son is tenaciously searching for the boy, using the church. He hasn't mentioned it to us, but Almond reported that he's raging about how the boy has to be Ashtart, and how he must be planning to seek revenge on him."

"If the nephew's identity is truly Ashtart, his grudge would be against the House of Mirchetta. He'd have no need to target Aileen and start a quarrel with me. I don't think we can be sure he and Ashtart are one and the same."

"I'd imagine the son is doing something terribly questionable. It should be quite obvious you wouldn't buy his claim that being half demon makes the boy the culprit and that we should just kill him... Apparently the demon who fathered him has already been killed."

Claude gives a brief sigh. "The cambion isn't necessarily Ashtart, but I'll keep him in mind."

"Please do. We may be able to use him for something. Oh, and I'll be returning Beelzebuth to guard duty soon. The village that was attacked has been largely restored, and the demons' patrols are working well."

Acknowledging Keith's report with a nod, Claude sets off again. Right now, frankly, he begrudges the time it's taking to walk through the corridors. "Did you learn anything regarding the attack?"

"The demons who are responsible are locals. They had no leader; they simply rampaged until they'd worn themselves out, then scattered. Beelzebuth nabbed a few and questioned them, but their memories seemed muddled. He couldn't get any coherent answers regarding exactly what had happened, or why they'd do such a thing. However, there was one concerning bit of information. They said there was a strange, cloying smell in the village at the time of the attack…"

"A smell?"

"We're looking into it," Keith tells him as he trails behind.

"How are the villagers responding to the demons?"

"Mostly favorably; it might be because our earlier response was good and fast. No one died, after all. The only ones making a fuss are the lazy son's hangers-on, the ones you cut loose."

"I won't change my policy."

"I didn't think you would," Keith says lightly. Then he makes a quiet suggestion. "We do want to profit from this, after all. Shall we add Mirchetta to your personal holdings, milord? The lacking heir to the duchy is up to all sorts of things, in addition to the matter of his nephew."

"That's an idea. It could be a souvenir for Aileen… Or would she dislike that sort of thing?" Claude smiles faintly.

Keith mulls it over. "She's able to tolerate almost anything, but I'm really not sure."

"Besides, I've shown her only a small part of what makes me the demon king." He's much crueler than she thinks he is. He's even more aware of this now that he's returned to human society as the crown prince. Ridiculous attempts to uncover the other's real intentions. Abrupt, calculating changes in attitude. A world in which the first one to betray the other wins. The anger that continued to smolder after he cast it aside sometimes threatens to flare up again. "I'll have to be careful not to frighten her."

"Good grief, milord, you're obsessed."

What is she doing now? The mere thought makes affection and keen longing well up inside him. So this is the distance humans live with.

I hope she's waiting quietly, but...

There have been no reports from the demons. In that case, he'll wait eagerly for her response to his letter, as a lover should.

After all, she's living under the same blue sky he can see through the corridor window.

My dearest Aileen,

There must have been times before this when I could not see you, yet having this distance between us makes the days seem terribly dreadful and unending. I can hardly believe I lived twenty-five years before I met you. I want to see your face. To hear your voice. I long to hold you. The clear blue sky pales in comparison with the light in your eyes. The comfort of the moonlit night is nothing next to the softness of your skin.

I also find myself growing uneasy in your absence. Do you still love me? It's no wonder you were angry at my decision to leave you. I had no idea that simply being unable to meet could cause such heartrending sorrow. It must have been the arrogance of my position as demon king. However, I beg you, don't misunderstand.

In your presence, I am but a man. Simply a foolish man who can no longer live without you, one who would rather let the world end than lose you.

Do you, a woman more noble than any goddess, feel as I do? I am impatient with myself for being unable to do anything but kneel and beg for your love.

Please, tell me you love me. Before I destroy the world in which I can't see you.

I await your response.

From Claude Jean Ellmeyer, to my beloved

★   ★   ★

"What's the matter, Aileen? I thought you had a report to make."

"Yes, Isaac... I did call you because I had a report. I'm about to make them add me to the student council, but..."

"You *what*? I told you to keep your head down, and then you just go and—!"

"Wait, I'll explain properly. Before that, though, we have a big problem. Almond just gave me a letter from Master Claude."

"Is he onto us?!"

"No, he hasn't figured it out yet, but... How am I supposed to respond to this?!"

Aileen's scream echoes in the sky.

There's a surprisingly small amount of sky lying between her and Claude, but he doesn't know that yet.

James Charles was the product of forbidden love between a demon and a human, and his very first misfortune was that his mother happened to be the beloved daughter of Duke Mirchetta. After she'd eloped with her demon lover, the House of Mirchetta had captured her and hired the church to kill his father. With her husband dead, his mother ran away to bring James to safety— at the cost of her own life. However, James didn't have time to grieve. His mother's younger brother—his own uncle—retained the seedy services of the church and made an attempt to kill him as well.

As he is a half demon, the demons were wary of him as well, and they refused to help him. Humans wouldn't accept a grubby half-human child, either. Hiding the fact that he is a cambion, James fled, desperate to try to grant his mother's final wish and survive.

Once he grew and skillfully blended into human society, as if to mock his pursuers, he entered Misha Academy as the top-scoring student and became president of its student council. He opted to stand out as much as possible in order to frustrate any potential assassination plots.

Like Claude, the final boss in Game 1, his character couldn't be romanced on the first playthrough. On every route, he became the final boss, destroyed Mirchetta, and died. Even on the second playthrough, when it was possible to romance him, he still became the final boss and seized control. Responding to Serena's love, the sacred sword destroyed only his demon side and made him human. Before it happened, though, Mirchetta fell.

If I'm going to save Mirchetta, I'll just have to keep him from changing into the final boss. Being saved by becoming human is a total cliché, but... Should I use the sacred sword to turn James? Would that really do it?

James is proud. *"You are our child, and we loved you even before you were born. Hold your head high, and please find your own happiness."* His parents had blessed him, and so he isn't ashamed of being half demon. Aileen isn't sure whether stripping him of his demon side would be the right choice.

Besides, he's useful precisely because of his unique pedigree. He'll come in handy in the future Master Claude intends to build.

Aileen wants to acquire this talent as is, no matter what. To that end, she has one broad plan of action: to do her utmost to keep James from becoming a demon.

James is being pursued by the church, and in order to defend himself, he uses magic and turns into a demon on several occasions. As a half demon, he becomes more like a demon both mentally and physically with each transformation, until finally, his humanity slips completely out of reach. At that point he's certain to become the final boss, and the duchy of Mirchetta will fall.

In the game, once he'd become a demon more than a certain number of times, the bad ending was locked in.

The in-game event she really has to watch out for is the swordsmanship contest at the school festival. During the contest, James falls afoul of the church's trap, and the fact that he's a demon is exposed.

And everyone who's due to take his life is on the student council.

"You're nominating Ailey Calois for general student council duties? You must be joking, Auguste." In the student council room after school, with the light at his back, James snorts derisively.

Auguste looks annoyed. He leans over the ebony desk. "It's not a joke. I was really impressed by Ailey's enthusiasm for improving this academy!"

"There's nothing more suspicious than a student who has that kind of enthusiasm on their second day here."

Inwardly, Aileen agrees: *You couldn't be more right.* However, she does think she wouldn't mind reforming the school while she's at it, and so she speaks up. "President James. It's true that I just transferred in, and I don't know the academy very well. It's also precisely because that's true that I can see things in a different light. I think I can be very useful."

"Exactly! Ailey's a transfer student, so he might be just what this place needs!"

"This academy is 'Little Mirchetta,' and the student council is 'the state in miniature.' In that context, this transfer student is someone from another country. What kind of imbecile would allow a foreign agent to meddle in their national government?"

"Oh, why not? I'm in favor. Let's put Ailey on the student council." Walt's spoken up from where he's sitting, chin braced on one hand, at a desk by the wall. Aileen looks over at him; she wasn't expecting support.

Auguste's face lights up. "Yes, Walt, exactly!"

"Besides, it's not uncommon to import exceptional talent from other countries. Right, Kyle?"

"It's a fact that the school festival preparations have left us short-handed. It would be a fine thing to have more like-minded comrades who want to improve the academy," Kyle Elford responds quietly.

Kyle is the only student council member she hadn't managed to meet earlier. He has rather Asian features, with black hair and pale skin. Like Walt, he's a slightly older character who acts as a treasurer; his taciturn nature makes him a good foil for the flamboyant Walt. Visually, they're quite striking together. When Aileen glances at them, Walt smiles at her, but Kyle doesn't even look up. He just keeps fielding paperwork at a terrific pace, his back incredibly straight. That stands out to Aileen as well.

Now I know for certain that all the love interests are here. Serena is key, though, and she isn't present... James, Walt, and Kyle are gathered in the student council room after school, but Serena has already gone home.

"That's three against one, then! Even if Serena vetoes it, it's still three against two, so that settles it, James."

"Putting decisions to a vote is stupid in the extreme. In the first place, Walt and Kyle are only shooting their mouths off." James is haughty, and he doesn't spare any respect even for the council's older members. However, Walt and Kyle seem to be used to it, and they don't get angry with him.

"You wound me. I did qualify that with 'exceptional talent,' James. We have a perfect matter pending right now, remember? Why not test him to see whether he really is exceptional?"

At Walt's suggestion, James's eyes widen. However, he promptly reverts to his composed, snobby expression. Before Aileen can ask him for details, he's rested his elbows on the ebony desk and laced his fingers together.

"—In that case, let's find out whether you really are an exceptional recruit with a genuine desire to improve this academy."

James is clearly planning to foist some sort of nuisance job onto her. Auguste looks rather uneasy. However, she'll never get anywhere if she backs down now, so Aileen accepts with a confident smile. "If it's within my powers. What do you want me to do?"

"Investigate. A month ago, a female student was injured. The culprit is rumored to have been a vampire."

"A vampire... You mean it was a demon?" Had that incident ever come up in the game? Aileen looks dubious. James nods, tapping his neck with a fingertip. "The student was unconscious, and there were two holes in her neck, as if someone had drunk her blood. The victim says she doesn't remember a thing, so talking to her is pointless. That's what provoked the rumor. I treated it as an accident and left it alone, but the Ladies of the White Lily caught wind of it. Oh, they're a parents' association made up of academy graduates."

She recognized the group's name from the game. Apparently the game's background elements existed in real life as well.

"They're all women, and they're very nitpicky—I mean, meticulous. They're extremely concerned that some sort of incident may happen before the school festival. The female student body of this academy counts many future noblewomen in their ranks. They say we can't wait until something happens to them before we take action."

In other words, some nagging parents are pushing for an investigation, but James thinks the rumor is trivial and doesn't want to deal with them. It's a pain, so he's hoping to make it Aileen's problem instead.

"From what I hear, since we haven't investigated the incident, they've gone to complain to the duke's proxy."

The duke's proxy. Aileen flinches, but although James is right in front of her and Auguste is standing next to her, neither of them notices.

"That's the demon king, isn't it? They're pretty brave..."

"I hear they're also planning to cross-examine him, just in case he's the culprit."

"I accept."

"Huh?"

"I said I'll take the job. I just have to investigate and hand over the culprit, correct?"

They suspect Claude of attacking a female student. As his fiancée, she can't let this slide.

James seems to have picked up on the fact that she's quietly burning with anger; his eyebrows draw together slightly, but he clears his throat and nods. "I leave it to you, then. If you resolve this incident, I'll put you on the student council, in charge of miscellaneous duties."

"I'd like that in writing, please. I can't have you saying you don't recall making any promises later on." She flashes an impudent smile. Behind her, there's a subdued burst of laughter from Walt. James sighs, then takes out a piece of paper and runs his quill across it. He writes in a practiced hand. Both the text and the format are perfect. She sees why this place is known as the state in miniature.

"One more thing. I think we'll need security, both to aid in the investigation and to prevent crime. I'd like to request the establishment of a guard unit as well."

"A guard unit?"

"Give us permission to carry swords, if you would. That'll be particularly important if the culprit turns out to be a demon like the rumors claim. It will also serve as a performance for the Ladies of the White Lily, you see?"

James rests his chin on his fist, thinking. "A security detail... Assuming you are the captain, what will you do for the rest of your team?"

"I'll put out an open call for volunteers."

That honest answer provokes a taunting smile from James. "Very well. I'll allow it. Assuming you get any applicants, that is."

"Thank you very much."

"All right. Regarding the establishment of the guard unit, then, here is your first task." James has been writing something besides the contract. He signs it, stamps it with his personal seal, then smoothly spins the paper to face Aileen.

It's a report about the new guard unit, including a rough summary of what they've just discussed. He wrote this while they were talking? Inwardly, Aileen is amazed: His facility for processing information is impressive.

"Take this to the principal of the academy—in other words, the proxy duke—and get his consent."

"...Pardon? The principal is the proxy duke?"

"For generations, Duke Mirchetta has also served as the principal of Misha Academy."

"Huh?!" She hadn't known that particular bit of information.

I—in other words, Master Claude is the current principal... Wait just a minute! Does this mean he may put in an appearance here in some official capacity?! If we happen to run into each other—!

Aileen shivers. James snorts. "You're about to investigate a vampiric incident that may be the work of a demon, but you're afraid of the demon king? All that spirit you showed was just an act, then."

"Th-that's not...true..."

"Naturally, we'll need the principal's signature and seal in order to establish a new organization. Of course, you don't have to go if you'd rather not. Although that will mean we never had this conversation." James smiles, holding the contract lightly between his fingertips.

If Master Claude finds out about me, he'll send me back immediately!

She's disguised as a boy, so she'll be fine—no, she can't rest easy with such a naive thought. He'll probably see through it. She's positive he will. Actually, if he didn't recognize her when she was standing right there in front of him, that would be a problem in its own right.

No, that's not the issue right now! What should I do...?

Her wandering gaze registers a motley collection of objects piled messily in a corner of the otherwise neat room. They might be props for the school festival. *Oh.* Her eyes widen in surprise.

"Well? What will you do? Will you go ask the demon king for his seal, or not?"

Aileen reaches out for the document on the ebony desk. Mustering up her strength, she grabs it.

She'll fool him no matter what it takes. Even if he is the demon king. Because she loves him.

"—I'll go."

Once again, the day has been busy since it started. "I don't suppose there's a way to make Aileen into a hug pillow," Claude mutters, his expression serious.

"I've learned something recently: When you're tired, milord, your thoughts invariably turn toward the bedroom, don't they?"

"I don't think I've managed to get the scent of yesterday's perfume off yet..."

"And it's made you miss Lady Aileen even more, hmm? Those ladies were so powerful it makes one question the inclusion of 'lily' in their organization's name... Still, you performed admirably as always, Master Claude. Victory was yours in an instant." Piling new documents on Claude's desk for approval, Keith gives him a thumbs-up.

With a deep sigh, Claude picks up one of the papers. "It was merely a consultation. There's no victory or defeat to be had."

"What are you talking about? You overwhelmed them with your face. It was far too persuasive. If someone with that face tells you 'I have no reason to attack a female student, nor any need to,' there's nothing to do but agree... Wow, is that irritating or what."

"I wouldn't do a thing like that when I have a fiancée. What objection could you have to that?"

"I object to that face, which decided the match for you the moment you stepped into the room. The Ladies of the White Lily were little more than giddy young girls before you! Well, it's better than being suspected without cause. Not that it solved much of anything."

"The vampire incident, hmm? Considering when it happened, I suspect someone took advantage of the Ashtart commotion and did it for the thrill."

"If it's Ashtart himself, terrific; let's get out there and capture him! After all, we still haven't managed to locate him, and on top of that, absolutely nothing is happening."

This is another major problem that's been worrying Claude.

"It's good that nothing's happening. However, everyone is beginning to relax and assume the warning was a sham. The thought that he's planning to make a move the moment I go elsewhere makes it impossible to return to the capital."

"When you look at it that way, it does make one think it might actually be connected to the struggle over the title of crown prince, doesn't it?"

"If things go on like this, I won't be able to see Aileen. Don't you think the situation is dire?"

"Why not split yourself in two? Luc was saying single-celled organisms can do it!"

"I've been sensing spite in everything you say for a while now..."

"Well, I'm tired too, you know. Take a break and let's have breakfast, shall we?"

The sun is already at its zenith, and the bells have struck noon. He can't find the energy to point out that this will be lunch, though. Keith says he'll get something ready and leaves the room, and he simply watches him go.

If he doesn't eat proper meals, Aileen will be angry with him. He's thinking about this absently with a wry and weary smile when there's a knock at the door.

"Come in."

He promptly retrieves the list of scheduled visitors from the depths of his memory. He recalls a Misha Academy student is due to make an appearance. However, his mind freezes up, completely unprepared for what walks through the door.

The visitor who's just entered is an enormous duck that's sprouted two human legs.

"……"

The duck's ample behind has gotten stuck in the doorway. It flaps its wings, successfully extricating itself, then waddles up to the desk. Briskly taking a document from under its wing and placing it on the desktop, it holds a stack of thick sheets of paper up to him, as if it's going to launch into a picture-card show. The papers hold sentences made of letters that have been clipped from newspapers and books.

SIGN AND STAMP THIS, PLEASE.

After reading the paper, Claude wordlessly looks down. The document in front of him has the sign and seal of the Misha Academy student council president on it. At the very bottom, there's a box for the principal's seal of approval.

…I just need to sign here and mark it with my seal, then.

Sorting everything out with an oddly calm mind, Claude puts his quill to work.

The huge duck watches him closely.

"……"

"……"

"…Why are you a duck?"

He really doesn't understand any of this, and so he decides to just ask. At that, the duck dexterously flips through several papers, then thrusts one out at him. Apparently, it had foreseen this question and has an answer prepared.

I SLIPPED OUT OF THE SCHOOL FESTIVAL PREPARATIONS TO COME HERE.

"…So there's a student in there, then?"

When he asks that, the duck seems oddly flustered. It flips through several more sheets, then shows him the answer.

No, I am just a duck.

"I see. I really don't know if it's wise to give documents to someone who's just a duck, though."

The duck is the messenger of Misha Academy.

"…The symbol of Misha Academy is a lily, the emblem of the Maid of the Sacred Sword. It isn't a duck."

"Master Claude! Aileen's response is here!"

Hearing that voice outside the window, Claude turns around. It's a crow demon with a bow tie around its neck. *Almond.* Before he stands up, he hastily stamps the document with his seal. However, he does check, one last time. "So I can leave this with you?"

The duck nods several times, and Claude hands over the document. The duck was the one who brought it, and therefore, he tells himself, it makes perfect sense to let the duck handle the rest as well.

"I think combining deterrence and furthering the investigation by establishing a guard unit is a sound idea. Give it your best."

Thank you very much.

Successfully getting through the entire conversation with its stack of papers, the duck waddles out of the room. Immediately, Claude looks over at the window. Almond unlocks it by himself and enters.

"It's from Aileen, is it? Good boy, Almond."

"I delivered right on time! I'm a clever demon! Demon king is happy, too!"

Claude smiles and strokes Almond's head, then takes the letter that's been tied to his leg. He can't treat it carelessly, so he breaks the seal with a letter opener, impatient. In that moment, it gives off the fragrance of a sophisticated perfume, making her image rise in his mind.

This really is a lovers' trial. Could one call it a long-distance romance?

Torn between two opposing impulses—the desire to bask in the fragrance a little longer and his impatience to read the letter—Claude gently unfolds the paper.

Dear Master Claude,

I am fine. Good luck at work.

Aileen Lauren d'Autriche

"Confuse him by wearing a duck costume; then distract him with my letter: a perfect strategy, if I do say so myself."

By the time she stops for breath and wipes the sweat from her forehead, a torrential rain is falling. Aileen, who's stuffed the costume into a bag in the shadow of a building, grimaces at the rain. It just keeps getting stronger.

"That response letter may have been ill-advised... I got the seal of approval, though, so that's all right." Now she'll be able to set up her guard unit. If she does, the way she can maneuver will change dramatically. It's a major step forward.

That was Aileen's carefree belief, but the rain continued falling for three days and nights. Almond lamented, "Demon king is so unhappy... You liar... I won't believe you ever again." Finally, when she heard the unending rain was threatening to make the nearby river overflow its banks, Aileen wrote another letter, under Isaac's supervision.

This response, the product of Aileen's agony, brought back the sun. By a curious coincidence, that night was the first time their guard unit went to work.

"I'd rather not run into Master Claude again for a while...!"

"Well, sure. If he finds out you sneaked in here, we could end up dealing with a volcanic eruption instead of a lot of rain." Isaac, carrying a lit hand lantern, is the first one out of the dormitory. He's wearing a hastily improvised armband that marks him as a member of the guard.

"That's not why! I mean I'm not happy about being compelled to write that mortifying letter, all about how I also wanted to see him again as soon as possible and how lonely I'm feeling!"

"Wow. It rained so hard the river almost flooded, and you're still saying that?"

"Th-that might not have been my fault..."

"We can hope, huh. Whatever you do, though, *do not* tell the demon king somebody made you write that letter." Isaac's eyes are very steady, so Aileen grudgingly stops arguing. However, inwardly, none of this sits well with her. *Almond's sulking and won't come out! The other demons, too. They're still keeping the fact that I'm here secret from Master Claude, but since all I did was answer a bit irresponsibly, I don't see why they have to be so—*

The demons are grieving along with him, and they blame Aileen. It isn't fair. Love can be quite the burden.

"And? The renowned Misha Academy guard only has two members?"

"Come now, I obviously plan to recruit more."

"...It's kinda late to be saying this, but could you not talk like that while dressed like a boy? My mind can't handle the confusion between what I'm seeing and what I'm hearing."

"Right. Sorry. There's no telling who might be listening. I'll watch it."

"...When I think about the fact that it's you, hearing you talk like that is really strange, too."

"Never mind, let's just go. The patrol comes first."

Misha Academy has a dormitory for students who've come a long way to attend the school, which means there's a curfew. That makes it easy to spot suspicious students who wait until after lights-out to act, or students who stay at the school instead of going home.

"By the way, how's life in the dormitory treating you? I wouldn't have minded sharing a room with you, you know."

"Don't give the demon king any more reasons to kill me, please. Life's much more peaceful if we have our own rooms... Listen, this school does have its own security already, right? You sure there's any point in patrolling?"

"If we find anyone before security does, we can question them about what they're doing. In particular, the student who's attempting to make demon snuff may try something."

"...Demon snuff. Right. I'm really not convinced there's any such thing, you know," Isaac says from up ahead. Aileen follows, keeping an eye on their surroundings.

"There's the vampire incident as well. We can't be certain it had no connection to Ashtart."

"You think? A demon issues a statement saying he's going to destroy Mirchetta, then goes and attacks a girl at the academy? What kind of joke is—?"

Isaac stops in his tracks. He motions for her to stay quiet, and she nods. They take cover in the shadow of a school building, and he quickly puts out the lantern. Isaac may say all sorts of things, but he is trying to carry out the sort of patrol Aileen wants.

They squint in the moonlight, managing to make out two shadowy figures. They're standing among the trees, apparently holding some discussion. When the girl takes a step forward, her profile comes into view, and Aileen blinks. "Rachel?"

"You know her? ...Oh right, she's the girl you saved on your first day here, huh."

"Wait, please wait! This isn't what you said earlier." Rachel raises her voice. The shadow beyond her turns around— It's big. A man.

So the rumor that she's been meeting a man was true. Don't tell me we've walked in on a tryst...

In that case, had her fiancé's anger been justified? No, even if that is true, there can't have been any need for punching and kicking. While these things race through Aileen's mind, the conversation goes on.

"Y-you said you'd help her. That's why I..."

"And what? You know full well that I did help her."

She recognizes that voice, and she very nearly leans forward. It's the underhanded arithmetic teacher who tried to make an example of her for not having her textbook the other day.

"Well, well. That's Professor Koenig."

She claps a hand over her mouth to keep from crying out. A voice has spoken behind them without warning, and Isaac pulls back, startled. Meeting both their gazes, Walt gives a devil-may-care smile and lightly raises a hand. "Hello, guards."

"W-Walt...! What are you doing here?"

"Student council members can join the new guard unit, can't they?"

"Monitoring us, huh?" Isaac mutters. The remark is brief, but it doesn't get past Walt.

"You could say that, I suppose. Never mind that for now. Eyes over there— Doesn't that look like the truth behind the vampire incident?"

"That girl was able to break off her engagement to the boy she hated. What on earth is there to complain about?" the professor asks incredulously.

"Her engagement was broken off because everyone said she'd been tainted by a demon and no one would go near her! They say her family may very well disown her!" Rachel exclaims.

"What of it? That's nothing. If she doesn't like it, she should simply have obeyed her fiancé in the first place. Even if he struck or kicked her."

"You can't be serious…"

"Well? How about it? Are you going to pay up or not? I don't mind publishing this letter."

"No, don't! If you do that, she'll be expelled!"

"Then just tell the truth. Tell everyone you requested this vampiric incident and that you're the real culprit."

Looks like we've solved the mystery all at once. I don't feel at all happy about it, though.

"All right, should we take those two in as the criminals?" Walt asks nonchalantly.

Aileen glares at him. Isaac sighs. "So you knew, huh, Walt."

"No, that's not true. I'm quite surprised. By the way, who're you? Ailey's friend? You transferred in at the start of the autumn term as well, didn't you?"

"You could just look that stuff up," Isaac goads him, neatly dodging the question.

They'd made sure to establish a justification for Isaac and Ailey's relationship. Ailey was the son of an upstart merchant, while Isaac's father was a man of property who'd loaned the merchant money. The two of them had known each other for ages, and according to their script, they'd met again at the academy by coincidence.

Meanwhile, Aileen is convinced that Walt isn't just there to watch them. *Does he suspect us? In that case, Kyle will, too. After all, if it's like the game, they're— No, never mind that for now. Rachel comes first.* She refocuses her attention on the other two. Rachel has just held out some paper bills and coins. She's trembling. Koenig counts them, then breaks into that nasty smile of his.

"Not enough."

"I-I'm sorry. I couldn't get a good price for my dress... I'll g-get it for you right away, though. Please give that letter back."

"As if I could! I return the letter now, and you'll just pretend you've got nothing to do with this."

"N-no, I won't..."

"I'm a generous soul, though. I could give it to you."

Rachel looks patently relieved.

However, Koenig's eyes are narrowed in a smirk. When Aileen sees that, she slowly reaches for the hilt of the slim sword at her waist.

"If you'll trade me your body, that is."

"Huh?"

He grabs Rachel's wrists, pulling her to him. She gives a little shriek. Leering, he covers her mouth with a handkerchief. Immediately, although Rachel's been struggling, her eyelids start drooping.

"When you wake up, you'll only have been attacked by a vampire. It will all be tidied away as the work of demons— Gwaugh!"

Without warning, Aileen has darted out of the shadows and kicked Koenig hard enough to send him flying. His attention had been entirely focused on Rachel, and he soars helplessly off to the side, but he springs to his feet again almost immediately. He's impossibly nimble for someone his age.

Then he promptly makes a break for it.

"Isaac, take care of Rachel!"

"M–Master... Ailey...?"

"Yeah. I figured you were gonna do that. Don't try anything stupid."

Once she's confirmed Isaac is tending to Rachel out of the corner of her eye, she takes off in pursuit of Koenig. She cuts through the dense trees of the vast rear garden, following the loud, rustling her target leaves in his wake. However, that rustling seems to be getting farther away, and at an incredibly fast rate to boot.

Koenig is a man, and although Aileen's confident in her athletic abilities, she's a woman. It wouldn't be too surprising if she couldn't match him in raw speed. Even so, how can he have pulled ahead this quickly? He's *too* fast.

And there's some sort of weird, sweet smell...

No, it couldn't be—demon snuff? In the game, demon snuff was described as cloyingly sweet. It also worked on humans. It enhanced their physical abilities, bringing them closer to demons. Koenig can't have— Just as the possibility crosses her mind, the bushes rustle, distracting her. She can hear someone else running away. The footsteps are light; it's probably a woman.

However, that sound is drowned out by a scream from another direction. "Wha, waaaaaugh!! Monster!!"

It's Koenig's voice. Aileen has absolutely no idea what's going on. Instead of following the fleeing individual, she forces her way through the brush in the direction of the scream. Suddenly, her vision clears. Under the moon, a figure sways lightly, then drops the unconscious Koenig onto the grass.

In this light, the figure's silver hair has a blue cast. A pair of horns sprout from his head. Black wings extend from his back. His eyes are red, just like the demon king's. In the moonlight, the diabolical figure is as beautiful as a fallen angel.

However, Aileen recognizes both that figure and this scene.

It's identical to the art of an iconic event.

James?! Why has he transformed?! This smell… It really must be—

The demon takes a wary step back, putting some distance between them. At the same time, she hears someone pushing through the brush behind her. The only one who would come here at this point is Walt. A realization hits her, and she gasps.

It's the event on the Walt route! The first battle with James!

"Pursuers are coming! Run, hurry!"

If James fights and is wounded here, he'll have to use magic to heal himself, and his transformation will advance. James's head comes up as if she's startled him. However, in the next moment, he takes to the sky.

Immediately afterward, a gunshot rings out behind her. The bullet whirs past Aileen, chasing the demon's receding figure.

"…Did you just let a demon go?"

"What are you talking about, Walt?"

Walt steps out into the moonlight. He doesn't even try to hide the gun he's just fired. Still smiling, he walks up to Aileen and grabs her by the shirtfront. She thinks he may be about to point the gun at her, but instead he rips her jacket open, sending uniform buttons flying and exposing her bound chest.

She tries to cover her bosom, but Walt shoves her to the ground. Even so, he doesn't miss that futile gesture of hers. He shoves the gun to her forehead, his eyes narrowing. The tip of Aileen's sword gleams at his throat.

"So you really are a girl... Who are you? Tell me. Depending on your answer, even if you're human, you won't get off lightly." His honeyed smile hasn't changed, but his tone is low and deadly serious.

Stay calm, Aileen tells herself. She smiles back at him fearlessly. It's going to be fine—she has something to bargain with. "The church's investigative powers are nothing to write home about, I see."

"What was that?"

"I know who you are. You're one of the Church of Mirchetta's cleaners, a so-called Nameless Priest. You've been raised secretly by the church and bolstered with regular administrations of demon snuff in order to put you on equal footing with the demons you hunt. That blessed gun you're holding is proof." She glances at the weapon in Walt's hand. Blessed guns are special weapons that shoot silver bullets purified with holy water. They're powerful enough that a single shot will kill a low-ranking demon.

"My, my. You're certainly well-informed. Although anyone who's in the know could tell as much from a glance at this gun."

"Kyle was sent to the academy with you."

Walt's eyes widen. Aileen continues reeling off game knowledge, as if it's information she's found out on her own. "You're both brilliant, the youngest Nameless Priests in history. The church has sent you here together, talented as you are, because it's been informed that a high-ranking demon it's been hunting for years is hiding at the academy. It's also possible that demon snuff is being used here. Am I wrong?"

"Who are you? Does Kyle know about you?" Walt repeats his earlier question, more carefully this time.

Aileen flashes him a knowing smile. "Would you release me?"

Realizing he won't be able to bludgeon her with secret information, Walt retracts the gun. Aileen closes her jacket with its remaining buttons, then gets to her feet. "Rest assured, Kyle Elford knows nothing about this. However, I haven't told anyone about your true identities. I don't suppose you'd reciprocate by keeping quiet about the fact that I'm a woman? Let's part ways on that note tonight."

"...Do you imagine that's enough to make me back down?"

"In that case, why don't you expose my actual identity, at least? After all, you are a Nameless Priest, someone who'd even kill an infant in order to put down a demon. Correct?"

The church headquartered in Mirchetta was one of the largest organizations in Imperial Ellmeyer. However, Aileen's father, Rudolph, wouldn't turn out counterfeit personal histories flimsy enough to be easily detected. Besides, if Aileen can get them to focus on her, it will be easier to keep James safe: He's the high-level demon they're after.

His face was still his own, so I think it's safe to assume he'll be able to return to his human form.

The fact that he ran away without attacking Aileen is proof he's still in his right mind. It should be all right.

"...You're the first woman who's ever spoken to me that sharply," Walt says, putting his gun away. The disheveled way he wears his uniform makes it easy to conceal the gun in it. "Fine.

I accept your terms. I doubt I'd benefit from spreading the word that you're female. On the other hand, if you make any noise about us or our mission, you'll alert the demon, and we can't have that. Our true identities can be our little secret."

"You're quick on the uptake. That's very helpful."

"And you're seriously brave. Even the clergy treat us like monsters. Just to confirm: Is that other student, Isaac, in on your game?"

"It doesn't look as though I'd be able to hide it, so yes, that's correct."

"It's wonderful working with intelligent young ladies. Everything goes so smoothly— And? What are you going to do with that teacher, *Captain of the Guard*?"

Aileen looks at the unconscious Koenig, then at Walt. His choice to overtly refer to her as captain is probably a signal to switch gears.

"Can I ask you to provide testimony about the conversation he had with Rachel?"

"Mm, that's a problem. I can't do that. I don't want anyone to know I was with you tonight."

The way he phrases it sounds suspicious, but he probably means that if the demon puts the clues together and deduces Walt's true identity, it'll make his job that much harder.

Aileen decides she should compromise.

"All right. Let's go back to Rachel, then."

"Huh? Are you sure? You're just going to leave the teacher? It does look like he's merely unconscious, but..."

"If only Isaac and I testify, he'll either talk his way out of the arrest somehow or say things about the demon. Besides, we wouldn't be able to protect Rachel that way."

Walt looks startled.

"Why don't you take a harder look at Professor Koenig, Walt? The way he was moving was clearly beyond what any regular human could do. You might turn up something interesting. Like demon snuff, for example."

"Oh... No, it's fine. We were letting this guy run loose on purpose."

"...Is it okay to tell me that?"

"It's not exactly important information. All right, my dear Ailey, shall we go back to Rachel?"

The endearment makes her scowl for a moment. When he sees that, for some reason, Walt laughs. "That reaction of yours... Does that mean Ailey is quite close to your real name?"

"That's an excellent question."

"What a cold reaction. We know each other's secrets and everything."

"Mm-hmm."

Deciding that paying any more attention to him will just be a waste of time at this point, Aileen starts back the way she came. Walt follows her. For some reason, he seems to be in a good mood.

"My friend's fiancé was striking her, and I wanted to help her."

In Aileen's dorm room, holding a cup of hot milk, Rachel starts to tell her story.

Isaac is sitting in a chair the wrong way around, his arms hugging its back. "By 'friend,' you mean the victim in the vampire incident? In other words, that was all a charade?"

"...I think that's...probably what you'd call it, yes."

"You're not being real clear. The teacher obviously did that on his own. Tell us about it."

"I-I'm sorry…"

"Isaac, stop that. You sound like you're trying to corner her… Rachel, would you tell us what happened, starting from the beginning?" She sits down on the bed beside the other girl.

Aileen's thrown her a rope, and although Rachel's been looking down, she raises her head. Then she gazes at Isaac, and at Walt, who's leaning against the wall. Finally, she looks at Aileen and begins to speak. "At first, it was only a complaint. I was also, um…in the same situation as my friend. Her fiancé had become addicted to this strange incense or something, though, and he was treating her more and more harshly. I couldn't bear to watch any longer. We tried asking Lady Serena for advice, but…"

Aileen feels her eyebrows twitch, but she keeps listening.

"As I was worrying, Professor Koenig spoke to me one day, out of nowhere… Um, he had come into possession of a letter my friend had written to Master Auguste…"

"To Auguste? Don't tell me it was a love letter…"

"D-don't misunderstand. Even if her fiancé was scum of the lowest order, my friend wasn't the type to betray him. She didn't even intend to send it. She merely put her adoration down on paper. I mean, to men, that may sound like nothing more than an excuse, but…" Rachel trails off.

Aileen nods. "I understand. I imagine she only wrote it to comfort herself, correct?"

"Th-that's right."

"And? Did he threaten to expose her for infidelity?" Isaac asks.

Rachel shakes her head. "No, he didn't. He refused to return the letter, but he said if things were that trying for her, he'd help us break off her engagement amicably. He said he happened to know about the strange substance her fiancé was using as well. He told me he'd advise her and wouldn't harm her, and so I told my friend about it. I also acted as a go-between, to set up the time and date. My friend went to speak with him, and…"

"____"

"I—I never dreamed it would turn out like this…" Rachel bites her lip; her eyes are damp with tears.

Sighing, Isaac prompts her to go on. "So? After that, naturally, you went to get some answers out of the teacher. Of course, he turned around and outright said you were an accomplice, and that if you didn't give him money, he'd make your friend's letter public?"

"Y-yes… My friend is practically under house arrest right now. Even I can't see her. I don't know what happened. It is my fault, though, and I at least wanted to atone for that. People are already avoiding her like the plague, and if that letter becomes public knowledge, her position will be even more…"

And that's what convinced her to try and buy back the letter?

I should have hit that teacher another five or six times. Is it too late to plunge him into hell at this point?

As Aileen plots, Rachel looks up. "No matter what my reasons were, I'm to blame. I'll accept my punishment. However, could you please avoid involving my friend in this?"

"C'mon, how are we supposed to explain this without a victim? It's not even possible. Are you stupid?"

Rachel makes a noise, deep in her throat. Aileen glares at Isaac. "Isaac, a little tact? …Rachel, there's no need to worry. Neither you nor your friend are at fault here. There is a way to drop that teacher into hell all by himself; Isaac's just about to come up with it for us."

"Me? Why? Pain in the butt."

"If you don't come up with one, I will. A prompt, physical method—"

"Wait, fine, I'll figure something out... The teacher was probably after this girl in the first place, you know." Isaac puts a hand to his mouth and starts thinking.

That remark startles Rachel. Aileen nods, agreeing. "After all, if the victim had been his real target, he wouldn't have brought up that negotiation with Rachel. He would simply have threatened her friend directly."

"But first he asked for money. He had to have known a student wouldn't be able to gather too much. Still, even if it wasn't much money, he wanted it. In other words, he must be hard up."

"Correct. Very sharp. That teacher likes gambling. He's on a losing streak right now, and he's saddled himself with a monstrous debt. It sounds as if he's into a rather dicey drug as well. He could probably never have enough money." That answer comes from Walt, who's been listening quietly all this time. He's probably referring to demon snuff as a generic illicit substance since Rachel is present.

Isaac sighs deeply, rubbing the back of his neck. "Well, it'll probably work out. I am the son of a rich man, after all."

Rachel blinks in surprise. Aileen looks puzzled, too. "You're planning on buying that letter? There's no guarantee that will actually silence the teacher."

"It's not that hard. All we have to do is get rid of the letter, suppress any and all information about the incident, and make the teacher destroy himself." Isaac looks unconcerned, and Aileen falls silent.

He holds me back all the time, but when Isaac puts his mind to something, he generally takes it to extremes.

She'll remind him not to overdo it later... Although she doubts that would have much effect.

The next day, after school, the matter is settled.

"Here. The letter."

Isaac has brought the letter back as if it's nothing. "My subordinate is so capable it's scary...," Aileen mutters, meaning every word she says. "How on earth did you make this happen?"

"I flashed some money at him and asked if he fancied a game of poker. Once he'd built up a good string of losses, I said 'You know, that Rachel girl sure is cute,' and he bet the letter voluntarily."

"That teacher's good at poker. I'm impressed you managed to win." Walt has accompanied Aileen as if that's only natural. They've asked Rachel to meet them in this empty classroom as well, but she isn't there yet.

"Poker is a mind game. Considering what happened yesterday, he's probably still pretty rattled. He seemed on edge, like he had no idea where things stood. Besides, I'm good at cheating."

Note to self: Avoid playing poker with Isaac at all costs, Aileen thinks.

"Still, this sum... Isn't that about as much as a teacher would earn in a lifetime?"

"He's probably planning to skip out on it. Since he thought I was a student, he completely sold me short. He even stamped this promissory note with his seal for me. Even though all I have to do is sell it to a slightly disreputable acquaintance of mine."

"…A *slightly* disreputable acquaintance?"

"I say slightly because the collection is technically legal. Now even if we do nothing, the teacher's done for. If a debt collector shows up here, he'll be out of a job on the spot."

"Well, I suppose that will do… And? Did he say how he'd gotten his hands on that letter? Or anything about the demon snuff?"

"It sounds like he found the demon snuff with the letter. He used it once and realized it made him feel good; he didn't know anything more than that. And apparently he's run out. When I started asking him about it, he turned around and asked me what it was instead, and if I knew where he could get some more."

Aileen sighs, nodding. "According to Rachel, her friend was carrying the letter in her bag, but it disappeared at some point… And he found it with some demon snuff? What does that mean?"

"Beats me. By the way, when I sell that promissory note, it's going to bring in quite a bundle. What do you want to do with it?"

He's asking for her decision, even though it's money he won on his own. Isaac's often very thoughtful like that.

Before she answers, a shadow stretches out behind him. It's Rachel. Isaac hasn't noticed her yet. Deciding on a whim not to tell him, Aileen smiles. "I think you can do whatever you like with it."

"Oh yeah? In that case, I'll give some to the victim first. If her family really does disown her, she'll need all the money she can get. I'll do my best to spin the story so it sounds like the incident was an accident, but still."

"Well, well. You're a pretty decent guy, aren't you?" Walt seems to have noticed Rachel as well. He smiles smugly, and Isaac glares at him.

"I'd never get a good night's sleep if I took that money for myself. If you use money the wrong way, it destroys you... Then there's that girl, Rachel."

"You're going to return the amount she paid in blackmail?"

"First, I'm paying off the amount her family borrowed from her fiancé's family! Then she can cancel the engagement with a clean conscience. That other girl can dissolve her impending marriage arrangements, as well. Everything can be resolved properly this way. Forget complaining or writing love letters she doesn't plan to ever send; she should just have done this in the first place."

"Then do you want to go with her now? What do you think, Rachel?"

When she says that name, Isaac looks startled. He promptly clicks his tongue in irritation, looking embarrassed. "Anyway, I'll go cash this in. We'll talk about everything else later."

Typical Isaac. He instantly decided to beat a hasty retreat. Aileen is biting back laughter, but he doesn't even glare at her before he turns on his heel. He doesn't talk to Rachel, either. She just watches him go.

"Well, I'm happy for you, Rachel."

"Y-yes... But, um, there's no reason for him to do all that for..."

"Does trusting him make you uneasy?"

Rachel, who's been smiling weakly, bites her lip. She probably can't decide whether it's safe to believe in Isaac.

"I think, at this point, you probably tend to doubt men."

"N-no, that's not... You've saved me several times, Master Ailey."

Well, I'm actually a girl, Aileen thinks, but she doesn't say it. Instead, she speaks to her gently.

She doesn't want her to stop here.

"You don't have to worry about it. It would be stranger if you didn't doubt them. Somewhere in your heart, though, do remember that you only trusted the wrong fellow. After all, you may have been hurt by a man, but it was also a man who helped you."

Rachel doesn't nod. Instead, she clenches her fists—then looks straight at her.

"I wanted to be someone special."

It's a line from the game, and Aileen blinks. Rachel continues, earnestly. "I think that was why I wanted to save my friend as well. I wanted to become someone dashing like Lady Serena, someone who could help other girls... However, I was afraid to fight head-on, and I acted as the teacher's intermediary without doubting him. If I'd truly wanted to save my friend, I should have gone my own way and told him he was wrong, even if he punched or kicked me for it."

"It's not your fault. It's the fault of the people around you who don't listen." She darts an accusing glance at Walt, but he just ignores it.

"Even so. I'll bring up the dissolution of my engagement myself. Even if I pay back the loan, if I'm still weak, I'm sure nothing will change."

"Yes, you're right. That's a good idea."

"I want to be someone admirable. I don't want to keep a fearful watch on others' moods or to be timid. And so—if you don't mind, would you let me join the guard unit? I may not be able to

handle hard physical tasks, but I'll do odd jobs or anything else that's needed."

Aileen is surprised, but she smiles. "Of course. You're welcome here. I look forward to working with you, Rachel."

"Yes, Master Ailey!"

"So you're member number four, then. Welcome aboard," Walt tells her casually.

Aileen frowns at him. "You're not going to tell me you're member number three, are you? I don't recall granting permission for that."

"Oh? What's this? We swapped secrets last night, didn't we?" Walt says, his words dripping with implication.

Seeing Rachel blink at him, Aileen sighs. "Very well. Here's a job for you right away, then: Go get permission from President James for the guard unit to use this empty classroom."

"Nothing could be simpler."

"Th-then I'll clean the room so we can use it! Let me go get the supplies!" Clenching her fists tightly, Rachel hurries out of the room in search of cleaning implements.

Once they're alone in the classroom, Aileen looks up at Walt.

"Come to think of it, what about Kyle? I just assumed you two would try to figure out who I was together."

"That's not even funny. Why should I have to do a chummy thing like that with a guy like him?"

Now that he mentions it, she recalls they didn't get along in the game, either. They each felt inferior to the other and considered themselves rivals. *That's not very efficient.* She shrugs, and then Walt peers into her face, coming too close for comfort. "I'll expose your secret all on my own."

"Curiosity can have fatal consequences. Step back, if you

would." Aileen has an elbow propped on the armrest and her chin in her hand, and as she warns him off, she doesn't even blink. While she's at it, she stamps lightly on the shadow at her feet. It's a signal to the demons that everything's all right. If Almond flies out, she won't be able to explain him away.

"'Step back, if I would,' hmm? I almost feel compelled to obey. That must be nice. I'm getting more and more curious about what I'll find if I expose your identity."

Ultimately, what he'll find is the demon king. That thought makes her feel sorry for him, and she switches back to speaking like Ailey. "In that case, give it your best shot."

"I plan to— And? How are you going to report this to President James and the Ladies of the White Lily? The easiest way to protect Rachel would be to call it the work of demons, but…"

Walt steps away from her. She likes how quickly he changes gears.

"I'll report that the criminal was Professor Koenig. Rachel had nothing to do with his nefarious activities. If I add a note to the effect that it would be best not to publish the full details, in light of their influence on the students, we'll be all set."

"I doubt Professor Koenig will conveniently keep quiet for you, though."

"We only have to wait until he's stopped coming to the academy to file our report."

In that case, the teacher won't be able to object. It probably won't take all that long, either.

"If President James says my report isn't solid enough even then, let's have the incident written up for the papers. I'm on very good terms with a skilled journalist."

When Aileen hints that Jasper is on standby in the town, Walt frowns. He probably doesn't want outside forces meddling with the academy while he's conducting his undercover investigation into the demon snuff.

"With regard to the Ladies of the White Lily, we'll make our report after Professor Koenig has been dismissed in disgrace. They'll settle for that. I'm sure they wouldn't want to see their alma mater dragged through the mud in the papers day after day."

"...True, ladies of that ilk loathe scandal. Ah, I see. The report is perfect. Still, I didn't expect that. I assumed a young lady with a sense of justice as well developed as yours would feel compelled to expose evil to the harsh light of day."

"Ciphers like that man don't matter. Besides, is Professor Koenig the true criminal behind this incident?"

Walt's eyes widen in surprise, and then he smiles without answering. However, that in itself is an answer. If it's no coincidence Koenig learned of Rachel and her friend's problem and obtained that letter, then she has some idea of who the real criminal might be.

Rachel and the other girl went to Serena for advice. Besides, someone else was there that night.

Naturally, the one who's supposed to stumble onto the first battle between Walt and James in his demon form is none other than the heroine, Serena. There's a very good possibility that the "someone" had been her.

Crossing to the window, Aileen looks out at the students below.

In the game, the demon snuff had been made from opium poppy analogues that grew wild on the school grounds. However, when Luc and Quartz had checked this morning, the poppies they'd intentionally left were still there, apparently untouched. She'd had Luc and Quartz infiltrate the academy as research students immediately after Claude took up his post as duke. If the poppies had been harvested, it had to have happened before then. That would mean the demon snuff had been made quite a while ago, and if so, it didn't match the time when demon snuff had first appeared in the game.

Don't tell me demon snuff is being sourced from the church and sold illegally...?

By rights, Koenig had nothing to do with the game. Had he gotten involved with the demon snuff because its source was different from the supply that was featured in the game? Walt and Kyle had suspected the teacher of using demon snuff but had let him run loose. That would make sense if they'd hoped to use him to find the one pulling the strings.

In the game, James is the one who resorts to demon snuff, but...

Who on earth has acquired it, and from where? What are they trying to accomplish with it?

Outside the window, Serena is laughing vivaciously with a group of girls—what is she planning to do with that other girl's letter to Auguste *this time*?

That question is answered the very next day.

During the lunch recess, Aileen manages to beat the crowd and snags a beef cutlet sandwich at the school dining hall, then heads for the guard room, which they now have formal permission to use. There's a crowd in front of the bulletin board, which is unusual. She's blinking at the sight when she hears someone sneer as they walk past her. "'To Kind Master Auguste,' huh?"

"Who wrote that thing? 'You appeared in my dream' and all that crap."

On the bulletin board, where the student paper and various notices are tacked up, the lovely stationery is clearly out of place.

That floral pattern—isn't that the letter that girl gave Serena?!

She hadn't written it so it could be exposed to the public eye and laughed at. Scowling, Aileen steps forward. "I'm with the guard unit! Everyone get away from the bulletin board!"

"Huh? Come on, what's wrong with looking at stuff that's been posted?"

Several boys who are two heads taller than Aileen block her way, smirking. Just as she comes up with a plan to put them all on the ground—

"Why are you making such a fuss about this nonsense?"

It's Kyle. With a dramatic tearing noise, he rips the letter off the bulletin board. Then he turns his cold gaze on the boys who are blocking Aileen.

"Can't stand tall unless you outnumber everyone else? You lot have no pride."

"L-let's go."

The smug boys exchange glances, then take to their heels. Kyle may be a simple treasurer on the student council, but he's notoriously good at hand-to-hand combat. In the game, there was an illustration of him knocking down multiple opponents simultaneously during a martial arts class at school. That's probably why the boys made themselves scarce. The ultimate source of his skill is most likely the fact that, like Walt, he's been trained as a Nameless Priest. In combination with his tall frame and quiet gaze, it makes him very intimidating.

As if he's taken the wind out of their sails, the onlookers scatter. Rumors are inevitable, but at least the letter's no longer on display. Aileen sighs with relief. "Thank goodness... Kyle, thank you very much for helping me. You're nice, aren't you."

"Nice? That's a grave misunderstanding." Kyle rips up the

letter. Then he looks down at Aileen with a slightly ironic smile. "A nice person wouldn't rip up a heartfelt letter as if it meant nothing."

"Huh? No, I think ripping it up was the best move."

"What?"

"After all, giving a thing like that back would have been crueler— Oh." Remembering that there had been a similar conversation in the game, Aileen falters for a brief moment. Wondering about the culprit's identity had distracted her, and so she hadn't noticed right away, but this is a game event on Kyle's route. Someone's love letter had been posted on the bulletin board; Serena had tried to put a stop to it and had ended up in a confrontation with the onlookers. Kyle had stepped in and saved her. Then he'd ripped up the letter and said the line he's just said to Aileen. However, Serena had gotten mad at Kyle for it; she'd gathered up the fragments of the letter and delivered them to its sender. Kyle had been drawn to her sincerity. It was what you'd call the initial flag event for his route.

B-but that's all right, isn't it? I should stay on friendly terms with him, and he doesn't think of me as a girl right now. In any case, it's not as if I want to romance him.

Thinking better of it, she smiles at Kyle, who's eyeing her suspiciously. "I do think you're nice, Kyle. After all, if you tear it up, the letter's sender won't have to worry about where it may have gone or ended up."

"…You're an odd one," Kyle mutters, sour-faced. Then he turns on his heel, and what Aileen sees once his back is to her makes her smile. *My, my. It really is just like the event,* she thinks. Beginning to feel a bit mischievous, she follows him.

Naturally, Kyle notices right away. He looks back at her

dubiously. "Why are you following me? You have no business with me."

It's the same line as in the game. Feeling rather moved, Aileen smiles at him. "I wanted to see the kitty behind the church, too."

"Wha...!"

Kyle gapes at her, looking as if he's wondering how she knew. Then he grits his teeth and faces forward again. "—I have no idea what you're talking about."

"I can see the cat food sticking out of your pocket."

"Th-this is..."

"There you are, Aile— Oh. Kyle, it's you."

Just as she's nodded to him politely, Walt comes running up. At that, Kyle's expression promptly reverts to normal.

"What happened?"

"...Ah. Well. I'm sure someone will tell you soon anyway, so I'll say it. Ashtart's sent a statement."

When she looks up, Walt's wearing a smile that doesn't go past his lips. Kyle frowns. "It was posted on the bulletin board by the rear door, of all places..."

To THE HUMAN FOOLS WHO REFUSE TO GIVE ME THE HEAD OF THE MAID OF THE SACRED SWORD: MISHA ACADEMY IS NEXT. I'LL MAKE IT RAIN BLOOD AT THE SCHOOL FESTIVAL. YOU'LL RUE THE DAY YOU DISOBEYED.

The report that Claude Jean Ellmeyer will be making regular visits to Misha Academy as its proxy principal for security purposes comes in right after that.

As one of Misha Academy's biggest events, the school festival is usually attended by crowds of people who aren't from the school, including academy alumni and residents of Mirchetta. Bustling with student performances and concession stalls, it takes place over two full days on a scale so grand that it could be considered one of Mirchetta's state festivals.

It also happens to be the stage for two major game events. One is the swordsmanship contest held on the first day. Participants compete to demonstrate their skill with a blade—fitting for the birthplace of the Maid of the Sacred Sword. The event would prove to be a troublesome one for James, though.

The swordsmanship contest is run by the church. They'll hide demon snuff in the grand prize, and James will be exposed as a demon.

The church is currently using Walt and Kyle to search for the demon lurking in the academy. However, they still don't know who it is. The lack of progress eventually makes them impetuous, and so they set a trap, completely neglecting the risk that students would almost certainly get caught in the middle. In the game, they'd very conveniently muddled their way through without causing any deaths, but James ended up surrounded by sword-wielding students and sustained a grave wound. Then, with his identity exposed and his back to the wall, he'd resorted to demon snuff and ordered the demons to wage war against the humans. In other words, this event would send him hurtling toward his transformation into the final boss.

Of course, if we can prevent this, I think there's a good chance we can keep him from going down that path...

The second highlight is the closing event: the ball where the Princess Lily White would be named.

This title goes to "the finest lady of the year," as chosen by the Ladies of the White Lily. In modern Japan, most people would simply call it a beauty pageant. In the game, the contest had been decided by simply checking character parameters, but in this new world, the Ladies of the White Lily screen the candidates, grading them on their etiquette and the like. The girl selected as Princess Lily White will receive a prize and the right to select her partner for the last dance at the ball. Whoever she chooses isn't allowed to refuse, and in the game, the event art changed depending on affection levels, so Aileen had tenaciously cleared every single route in her past life. What's more, this was also the place where the villainess had been condemned. An eventful gala indeed.

The ball being what it is, I'm also worried about Rachel, but... She'll be all right, won't she?

The favorite for Princess Lily White this year is Serena Gilbert. Rachel is also among the candidates, but like Aileen, she's been busy with her guard duties.

After all, the students have begun searching for partners for the ball.

"Huh?! What do you mean, you can't dance with me?!"

An angry yell echoes through the courtyard, drawing furtive glances. Blood has rushed to the boy's head, though, and he doesn't seem to care what sort of attention he attracts. "The insolence—you're just a commoner! And here I am, going out of my way to invite you!"

"N-now now, let's just calm down." Serena has already wedged herself between them, attempting to mediate. When they see this, expressions of relief appear on some of the watching girls. Serena turns to the girl who's received the confession, speaking to her gently. "I do think the two of you would make a good couple. Besides, you haven't settled on a dance partner yet, have you?"

"W-well no, but... But there's...someone I'd like to ask myself..."

"Auguste says he'll be busy during the festival and may not attend the dance."

Serena's artless revelation instantly makes the girl blush bright red. She works her mouth, opening and closing it several times, but she doesn't make a single sound. The glances directed at her immediately shift from sympathy to derision.

Oh goodness, she's after Master Auguste? She's aiming far too high. Unable to endure the scorn directed at her, the girl stares down at her feet.

"Maybe reconsider the offer. It would be embarrassing not to have a partner for the ball, wouldn't it?"

"Y...yes, I suppose so..." The girl seems like she might burst into tears at any moment. The irritated boy has been watching the exchange, and he grabs her arm roughly. "Nobody was going to ask an ugly girl like you to anything, and I felt sorry for you, so I did you the favor of— Gweh?!"

The boy takes a flying kick from behind and sinks to the lawn. Stepping on his back, Aileen makes a muffled declaration: "That is not how you ask a lady a question. Try again."

"M-Master Ailey! Please don't just dash out like that...!"

Rachel comes running like her life depends on it. She catches up to Ailey, then dons an admonishing expression. She's wearing her armband. "We're with the guards! Do not threaten or pressure female students under any circumstances! —Are you all right?" Rachel immediately approaches the girl whose arm had been grabbed.

Serena, who's been looking stunned, frowns. "Why are the guards— Wait, before that, why are you a duck?! Who is that?!"

"I am simply a duck and nothing more. I have no name."

"That voice... You must be Ailey Calois. Keep your antics in check, will you?!"

"Ailey? What in the world are you doing in a duck costume?" Auguste appears, holding a roll he's bought at the school store. At the sight of him, Serena's threatening expression promptly vanishes. She's an open book.

"I would rather not have people see my face at the moment."

"What, did you get injured? You're a man, so don't worry about things like that. Let me see—" Aileen's pointed her sword at Auguste, and he stops, raising his hands. "Y-you're very clever with that. You can use a sword with those hands?"

"This duck costume is surprisingly functional."

"...So the guard unit's so busy you have to work even when you're dressed like that, hmm?"

Inside the duck's head, Aileen sighs. "A lot of the male students are doing unpardonable things in their search for a partner for the ball. I've been jump-kicking quite a few offenders as soon as I spot them."

"I guess the school festival is just around the corner, isn't it? Oh, if you'd like, I'll help out."

"Would you take this boy to the guard room, then? There's a

fellow named Isaac on standby there, recording demerits for bad behavior."

"Will do. Oh right, I should mention: Serena, seriously, don't mediate in any way that might catch the attention of the guard unit."

"I—I only acted as a go-between because I was asked to." Serena glares, not at the smiling Auguste, but at Aileen. "As a transfer student, you may not know, but being alone at the final event of the school festival is terribly painful. I only stepped in for that girl's sake—and you don't know a thing about this, Auguste, so don't make me out to be the villain."

"Oh, erm... Right, I'm sorry."

"There's no need to worry about that. The guard unit has decided to accompany any unpartnered girls at the dance."

"Huh?"

Serena blinks. Aileen ignores her, looking at the girl who's with Rachel instead. "I'd like any girls who haven't found partners and are being pressured by boys to come speak to the guard unit first. We're bursting at the seams with pointlessly gorgeous members, and they'll serve as their partners to the best of their abilities. If you're willing, please dance with me."

"Huh...? M-may I...really...?"

"Of course. I am a little short, though; I apologize for that."

"M-Master Ailey, remember you promised I'd have the first dance with you!" Rachel puffs her cheeks out, pouting.

Aileen smiles at her—although, since she's wearing the duck's head, her face isn't visible. "I know. It's just that I'll need to help, too. It would be dangerous to leave too much to Walt, and Isaac's stamina isn't very good, so he says he can only handle five partners at most."

"Huh? I—I see... H-how many has he taken at this point?"

"Wow. That's a great idea. Count me in, too."

"Auguste?!" Serena sounds aghast.

Auguste gives a little laugh. "Well, I've been wondering what to do for a dance partner at the closing event. It might be better if I helped out this way. It's possible that no one will ask for me, but still."

"Wha—? Um, n-no, Auguste, you could have as many as you—"

"Thanks, Auguste! That's a great help!" Interrupting Serena, Aileen grabs Auguste's hands firmly. "Walt can fill you in on the details."

"I see, yes, Walt did say he was working as one of the guards as well." Nodding, he helps up the boy Aileen had been stepping on this whole time, then walks off. Rachel also leaves, escorting the female student back to her friends.

Aileen sees Serena clench her fists. This looks like an opportunity, so she puts out a feeler. "Auguste certainly is popular, isn't he? You know, the letter that was posted on the bulletin board the other day was addressed to him as well."

"...Oh, was it?"

"I saw the girl who wrote that letter give it to you to deliver."

Serena turns around, then forces a smile. "What? Don't tell me you're insinuating that I was responsible for that spectacle? So the guard unit even sticks their noses into matters like that..."

"No, I'm just trying to confirm the facts."

"From the way you're talking, it does sound as though you do suspect me. Even if you said I did it, though, I doubt anybody would believe you."

Aileen falls silent. Serena genuinely does have a strong reputation. The game's note that she's skilled at looking after others is true in this world as well, and the way she speaks her mind to boys has won her trust and adoration from the girls. She's also on the student council, and even the male students respect her.

Well, she'll do me no harm...but I don't like her methods.

Now, what should she do? Aileen is still silent, and the corners of Serena's lips rise in a smile. "All right. I'm busy, so I'll be goi—"

A commotion far louder than the earlier one starts up. Serena's eyes turn toward it. The moment she hears a voice say "demon king," Aileen dives into some nearby shrubbery. She picks up a couple of twigs her maneuver broke and disguises herself as part of the bush. She then strains her eyes to get a good look at the approaching figure.

Flowing hair that might have been cut from the night sky. A perfect physique seemingly modeled on the golden ratio. A bewitching face that dazzles both men and women, anchored by red eyes that shine in a somber, wistful way. And that alluring voice gripping the attention of everyone who can hear it.

The students freeze as if they're frightened or perhaps hopelessly fascinated.

Master Claude...

She hasn't seen him in quite some time, and her heart flutters. This is no time for palpitations, though. If he finds her, he'll instantly send her packing. That's why she's disguised herself twice over, first as a boy, and then with the duck costume. Even she doesn't understand it, so no doubt Claude won't either.

Parenthetically, when she'd told Isaac about this plan, he'd made fun of her: "When it comes to the demon king, you get way too dumb." Luc had lamented, "Love is a fearful thing," and Quartz had given her some off-target advice: "If you adorn yourself with flowers, you'll be charming." Aileen wishes they'd show a little more consideration for the trouble she goes through.

"It's a spacious academy. I'd expect no less from such a distinguished school," she hears Claude say. He sounds impressed. James is showing him around, and he's brought Keith and Beelzebuth along.

"The students are well-mannered, too. I was wondering what we'd do if they threw rocks at you for being the demon king."

"Sire. Your next meeting is coming up. We're short on time." Beelzebuth, who's dressed in a sharp military uniform, takes out a pocket watch. *Beelzebuth*. Aileen is so moved she almost tears up.

He's able to read numbers properly...!

Not only that, but he's even using a pocket watch and managing Claude's schedule. What marvelous progress.

"At this point, I've only shown you half of what there is to see. Is it already time for you to go?"

"No, do continue. The school festival is fast approaching, isn't it? I'd like to get a solid grasp of how the grounds are laid out. The question is how they'll go about mounting an assault on this place, if it comes to that."

"They couldn't assault it. No demon could possibly be a match for you, my king," Beelzebuth replies simply.

"Then why has Ashtart declared he will rise against me and go against my wishes?"

"Well, erm..."

"Set your biases aside and think, Bel. I'm confident that you can do it."

Claude is instructing Beelzebuth. This when one member of that pair was so overprotective, and the other so thoughtless.

Keith, who seems to be feeling just as moved as she is, gently pinches the bridge of his nose.

"Now that you mention it, there was something I wanted to ask you. Is there a duck at this acade—?"

"President James! You haven't had your lunch yet, have you? If you like, I'll take over for you!" Just as Aileen flinches at the word "duck," Serena dashes out right in front of her. Softly, she places a hand on Claude's arm.

Wha—?! Wha, wha...

"Serena Gilbert. Are you sure?"

"Yes. Oh, but have you not sat down for lunch yet either, Principal? If so, I'll show you to the dining hall. Their offerings are truly delectable." Serena looks up at Claude, her cheeks flushed.

Wait just a... Hold it. Don't you idolize the Maid of the Sacred Sword, Serena? That's the demon king, you know?! The Maid's enemy! Are you sure?! What about Auguste?! Aileen wants to grab her by the shirtfront and shake her, right this minute... But she can't.

Claude looks at Serena steadily, sizing her up. Then his eyes abruptly sharpen.

"Bel, you go back."

"Understood, sire."

"Keith, you go as well. Handle the meeting. I'll look around the academy with her a little while longer."

"Huh? Well, all right, but..."

"Thanks for your help. Now then, Secretary Gilbert."

"Please, call me Serena," Serena tells him gaily, and Claude nods.

"All right, Serena. Please continue the tour."

"O-of course. Leave it to me. This way, please... Um, you are only standing in for the principal, aren't you? Would it be all right if I called you by your name, Master Claude?"

Serena fidgets, looking up at him through her lashes. The twigs Aileen's holding snap.

Claude's face remains perfectly composed. "Yes, that's fine. However, refrain from saying it too sweetly, if you would."

"Sw-sweetly? Oh, I'd never..."

"My fiancée is surprisingly jealous, you see."

As if he's remembered something, Claude smiles very faintly. Serena's face turns such a deep red Aileen almost swears she can hear it happen. At the same time, screams go up here and there, and multiple female students swoon. Even Aileen, who should be used to this, writhes and sinks to the ground. It's been too long. As always, that face is a weapon. It might be best to hide it by making him wear a paper bag.

Where, and when, did I ever get jealous...?! Oh, curses. That's right. At the soiree where I signed the dissolution of my engagement! When I heard that Lady Lilia and Master Claude had spoken...!

If that reaction struck him as jealousy, she could hardly blame him. Frustrated, Aileen pounds the ground with her fists. One of these days, she'll have to explain to him properly that she isn't really so petty. She is going to become empress, after all. She's perfectly capable of accepting concubines... Although she feels rather conflicted about the idea of him turning that exquisite face toward someone who isn't her.

It takes her ten deep breaths to calm down, and by then, Claude and the others are gone.

When she stands up, the sudden appearance of a duck from the bushes startles the students.

He caused a misunderstanding there, though, didn't he...? Don't tell me...

Hoping this won't warp into anything complicated, Aileen— still in duck form—hurries off to administer a flying kick to yet another boy she's spotted harassing a female student.

Aileen's nasty premonition proves to be right on the mark.

"It's very possible that Ashtart's statement is a hoax, but the principal has kindly arranged for some knights to bolster security. He wants someone to act as a liaison between the knights and the academy."

"Here! I'll do it."

In the student council room, Serena raises her hand. Since this is a meeting, for once, everyone is present. James told Aileen at the outset "I have no recollection of assigning miscellaneous duties to a duck" and nearly kicked her out, so Aileen has grudgingly removed her costume. She frowns at Serena, who's sitting directly across from her. Walt is wearing a similar expression as he raises his hand. "I'll do it. This is a security detail, right? It would be dangerous for a woman."

What he says is reasonable on the surface, but he probably wants to get a better idea of the state of security for the sake of his demon snuff investigation. Kyle also nods quietly. "In the event of an emergency, it would be better if the liaison was male."

"This is only mediation. Besides, in an emergency, Master Claude will protect me, so it's fine."

"But he's the demon king, isn't he? You hate demons, Serena. They're enemies of the Maid of the Sacred Sword—"

"Auguste, no. Stop. That man is still human." Serena stands

up, interrupting him. "The Maid of the Sacred Sword would surely have tried to save even the demon king. With that in mind, although I refuse to side with demons, I do intend to ally myself with him."

That man. Him. It almost sounds like she's already on close terms with Claude. *I knew it. She's gotten the wrong idea... Maybe I should seriously consider hiding that face of his.*

From the looks of it, Serena has completely switched over from Auguste to Claude. *At first sight?* she thinks, but a moment is time enough for human emotions to change. Besides, Claude is fiendishly gorgeous. If he put his mind to stealing the heart of a rather sheltered girl, she'd never stand a chance.

"Women are shockingly fickle...," Walt murmurs, looking a little appalled.

Next to him, Kyle offers some advice. "Even if it is just acting as a go-between, it isn't a good idea to send a female student. The demon king has a fiancée. What if you offend Duke d'Autriche's daughter?"

Aileen opts to stay silent to head off any chance of her over-reacting. Any odd behavior here might betray her true identity to Walt.

James cocks his head, perplexed. "His fiancée's in the capital. I doubt there's any need to be quite that wary."

"Nooo, President. We really shouldn't be careless there. After all, this is the house of d'Autriche we're dealing with. Their progress, or lack of it, hinges on whether the demon king becomes emperor. I imagine they'll have a spy or two shadowing the demon king, just to keep an eye on him."

Never mind spies. The daughter of the household is here in person. However, she sides with Walt, playing innocent. "If his fiancée gets the wrong idea, it's bound to cause trouble for the principal as well."

"Oh, I don't mind one bit. That's exactly what I want."

Serena looks supremely confident as all eyes turn to her after her bold remark. James folds his arms, grimacing. "I hear Aileen Lauren d'Autriche has quite an unforgiving personality. If we get a complaint from the House of d'Autriche, it really will mean trouble for us. The emperor is about the only one who can stand up to that family."

"She might even barge in here herself. She's rumored to be an outlandish, preposterous young lady."

"Judging from the fact that the demon king didn't bring his fiancée, even though demons are threatening to attack and she holds the sacred sword, I imagine she must be quite a problematic individual."

Harsh personality, preposterous young lady, problematic individual. Since they couldn't meet the person in question, rumors and reputation were bound to shape their concept of her. That was inevitable... However.

You'll all live to regret this.

Auguste flashes a diplomatic smile, attempting to rein in the free-range comments. "We can't really know what sort of person she is when we haven't met her... Oh, but there was a portrait going around, wasn't there."

"A portrait?" Aileen's eyebrows rise sharply.

James nods. "Come to think of it, there was one in circulation a little while ago. If it's true to life... Honestly, I wouldn't touch that."

"I was impressed by how novel the demon king's tastes were. I don't want to emulate them, though."

"Really? I just assumed his preferences were out there because he's a demon. Made sense to me at the time."

"...What sort of portrait is it? I haven't seen it."

"I'm pretty sure I have it around here somewhere... Oh, yes, here it is."

Auguste has apparently been using the back of it as scrap paper; he spreads it out and shows it to her. Aileen snatches it away from him, takes one look at it, and is immediately rendered speechless.

Put briefly, the subject is ugly. An extremely long nose, a mouth like a slash. It's doubtful whether it's even depicting someone human.

I don't know who's been spreading this around, but they clearly have a death wish.

Aileen decides to have Jasper look into it, starting tomorrow. She has to erase these from the face of the earth. She folds the portrait carefully, buying herself time to stifle her anger. In front of her, Serena is making an impassioned speech. "But Master Claude is extremely handsome, isn't he! I'm convinced: The demon king's current engagement must be a plot by the House of d'Autriche! Poor Master Claude! Thanks to his jealous fiancée, he has no freedom. I want to aid him in his time of need."

"—I—I know how you feel, but, Serena... That doesn't really have anything to do with being the school's liaison."

"I'm going to invite Master Claude to the school festival. As soon as I'm chosen as Princess Lily White, I'll name Master Claude. I'd really like to ask him to attend as my partner, but he has his position as principal to think of, you know? And so—"

"Um, I need to head over to the guard post. We have to get ready for tonight's patrol." Aileen has let Serena's monologue go in one ear and right out the other. Looking at the wall clock, she gets to her feet. The sun is setting earlier these days, and it's already dark outside.

"Oh, that time already? I'll go as well."

James has risen from his chair. Aileen blinks at him. Everyone else is watching them, eyes wide. However, James is wearing his usual inscrutable expression. "Let's go," he tells Aileen.

This isn't good, Aileen thinks. *I'm supposed to go to Luc and Quartz's joint research laboratory to talk a few things over, but...*

Rachel isn't involved in the night patrols, so she isn't a concern. Aileen and Isaac have arranged to meet up at the laboratory, so they're moving separately. All that's left is for her to slip off on her own somehow, without arousing any suspicion, But...

"I was surprised by Serena."

"I heard that in the Far East, people often say this proverb: 'Women's hearts and autumn skies.' It's exactly like that, isn't it?"

"Kyle, what does that mean?"

"I've heard that before, too. I'm pretty sure it means their feelings change easily."

"Why are you following me, President James, Auguste, Kyle, and Walt?!" Aileen can't stand it anymore; lantern in hand, she turns and shouts at them. They all exchange looks.

"Well, I mean, listening to her go on about that would be sort of... You know what I mean, right, Kyle?"

"In any case, if the president isn't present, it won't be much of a meeting. What's the point if he's not there?"

The two older students are making blatant excuses. Fighting

back a headache, Aileen shoots a look at James and Auguste. "In that case, shouldn't the student council president and vice president have worked a little harder to put the meeting back on track?"

"I refuse. Doing pointless work goes against my principles."

"Erm, I'm not great at that sort of thing, either..."

Is the fact that Serena's the heroine rendering the love interests incapable of stopping her when she runs amok? What a sorry state of affairs.

"Hey, come on, Auguste, that's pathetic. Are you even aware that you've been dumped?"

"Huh? Was I?"

"The man in question's the only one who doesn't realize he's been discarded for another."

Walt and Kyle are laughing at Auguste. James mutters, looking rather disgusted. "As long as no one brings drama to the student council, anything's fine with me. I was just thinking it was getting to be intolerable."

"...Listen. I'm only saying this because we're all guys here, but... If this is about Serena, I don't think that's what happened. After all, it's not as if she liked me."

Auguste smiles in a vague way. Everyone looks at him, startled. Forgetting her irritation, Aileen pushes for details. "What do you mean, Auguste?"

"I stand out because I'm on the student council, and I also happen to be popular with some girls. That's why. I think she just assumed I was the most approachable one here, and that she had a chance with me."

"...I see. So she wanted a popular sweetheart who'd make everyone jealous? That sounds plausible. She does enjoy standing out."

Auguste doesn't deny Walt's analysis. He only laughs it off. That gives Aileen an idea of the game's progress. *In other words, she's trying to look good in front of everybody, and she hasn't actually romanced anyone?*

That was how beginners tended to play. In a game where a harem ending was possible, it might have been an acceptable strategy, but the *Regalia of Saints, Demons, and Maidens* series didn't have those. If this was where things currently stood, the possibility that Serena wasn't even on the Auguste route was very high.

"Does that also explain the way she's behaving around the acting principal as well, then? Ridiculous. She's dealing with the demon king."

James shrugs, and Walt laughs. "But he's also the crown prince. With looks like those, I can see why she'd be dazzled. Not only that, but he's the half brother of her idol Lilia Reinoise's fiancé."

"And also the fiancé of Aileen Lauren d'Autriche, whom she considers an enemy? ...She can't be planning to steal him, can she? Even in love, it's important to show restraint." Kyle grimaces at the thought of impropriety.

Auguste is frowning as well. "I'm bad with ugly domestic situations. What are you going to do about the liaison position, James?"

"You heard how noisy she's being about it. I'll just have to give her the post. Besides, I didn't say so right then and there because I assumed it would to go her head, but the demon king's requested she be the liaison as well."

Everyone looks startled. Aileen's brain stops working for a second. *What is Master Claude thinking? It can't be... Is he having an affair? And hiding it from me?*

She decides to set conditions regarding concubines as soon as humanly possible. At the very least, she refuses to accept Serena.

"I'll at least keep an eye on the security, to ensure there are no holes. That's why I've come along on the night patrol."

So it hadn't been to escape from Serena's impassioned speech? Aileen's tempted to ask, but ultimately decides not to. No doubt everyone has their reasons. Limiting herself to a single sigh, she starts forward. Everyone else follows her.

Auguste speaks up, seemingly enjoying himself a great deal. "Night patrols sure are fun. I don't think we've ever walked around together like this before."

"Now that you mention it, I believe you're right." Kyle nods.

James snorts. "It's merely coincidence. There's no need for pointless chatter."

"Who wants to get together with other men and talk anyway? Right, my dear Ailey?" Walt pointedly sets a hand on Aileen's shoulder, and she smacks it away coldly.

"How have you managed to keep the student council running if you never talk to each other?"

"We just...did, I guess?" Auguste cocks his head, perplexed, and Walt nods in agreement.

"It helps that we're all brilliant."

"As long as each individual task is performed correctly, it's only natural for everything to go smoothly," Kyle adds.

The two older students are very laid-back about the whole endeavor. Without thinking it through, Aileen breaks in. "That can't be why. It's because President James is a brilliant organizer."

"...What?" James says dubiously.

Aileen stops, turning to face him. "Groups fall apart unless someone takes on the task of holding them together. If all the members move without any regard for the others, absolutely nothing would get done unless the president, the person who's taken command, is an outstanding leader. I've only been part of the council for a month, but I actually do think you're amazing, President James. You assign each and every job very efficiently."

"...Compliments from you make me feel ill."

Even though she's praising him, he looks repulsed. Aileen shrugs. "Of course it's true that both the upperclassmen are outstanding in their own right, and Auguste's role in reducing friction is also vital. I'm not saying that President James is the only brilliant one. If each of you worked a little more closely with the others, though, I think the student council would be even better."

"Exactly, Ailey! You really know just what to say!" Auguste thumps her on the back vigorously, and Aileen almost chokes. Auguste apologizes with a cheerful expression that doesn't look the least bit apologetic before turning to the others. "Since we've got the chance, let's get along better from now on! You heard Ailey."

"...How strange. Hearing it come from you makes me want to do it less, Auguste."

"Huh?! Why?!"

"Because no one wants to be as simpleminded as you are," James says flatly. Auguste looks dejected.

Kyle lowers his eyes. "As long as we each carry out our own tasks, that's good enough. I'd prefer to be left on my own as well."

"You said it. There's nothing worse than having colleagues

who get in your way." Walt is smiling, but Kyle's eyebrows twitch at the passing comment. It's pretty obvious that they're rivals.

I swear. Why are men such children? Sighing, Aileen breaks in. "Oh, that's fine. It's better to be held back by others than to be the one who holds others back, isn't it?"

"...Bold words."

"So, why not just get along?" It was a casual proposal, but she's starting to feel good about it. She steals a glance at the other four. Walt and Kyle are assassins who've been sent on a mission to kill James, while Auguste has the role of ultimately destroying him. Every member of this group is here to kill or be killed by the others.

If they're friends, they'll go easier on each other. That's true even for James. If someone helps him, he probably won't feel so hopeless that destroying Mirchetta is the only choice he has left... What he truly needs is a place to belong. A place where he can live in peace and be himself, even if he's half demon. As long as he has that, he'll have no reason to lay waste to everything around him.

"Get along, hmm...? Well, true, we are dealing with a potential demon attack."

"Don't even joke about that. I refuse." With that, James sets off, pressing on ahead.

Walt spreads his hands in mock surrender. "You heard him, Ailey. Too bad."

"...Say, does anyone else smell something weird?" Auguste is looking around uneasily. Walt's face immediately sobers. "It's sort of sickly sweet... James!"

Up ahead, they can see James listing drunkenly. As he topples to the ground, Auguste and Aileen rush over to him.

"Hey, James! Are you okay?!"

"...I...I'm fine. Let me be...!"

The smell is unmistakably demon snuff. That has to be why James is acting strange.

But where is it coming from? No, more importantly—!

The bigger problem is that James is on the verge of turning into a demon.

"Auguste, take President James back to the dorm right now and let him rest."

"Y-yeah, good idea. C'mon, James."

"I'm fi... I can go...on my own."

"President James, getting away from here comes first. Hurry."

James glares at Aileen. Auguste has slung an arm around him to help keep him upright. "Don't tell me this is...your doing...!"

"Let's go, James. You've gone white as a ghost. You should hurry and lie down."

"Take care of him, Auguste." As she speaks, she touches James's chest lightly, as if pushing him away. She uses just a little of the power of the sacred sword. It's the same as when she restored Claude's humanity after he'd become a dragon: The demonic miasma is trying to drag him down, and she drives it away, using a burst of power as gentle as the wind.

It must have gotten easier to breathe. James looks up, startled. One more time, he murmurs: "You... Did you just...?" He looks as if he's not sure what he should say. However, Auguste helpfully drags him away.

"Would you go report in to the teachers as well, Ailey Calois?"

"Oh, Kyle, you don't need to bother about that. Not with this kid."

"What?"

"He knows who we are. He seems to be an ally from elsewhere."

Aileen has gotten to her feet, and Kyle looks her over from head to toe. She holds her head high, determined to not offer him anything to complain about. However, Kyle frowns and mutters to Walt. "When he's this delicate?"

"Well, you see, our dear Ailey's a— Oops, that's supposed to be a secret, isn't it?"

"…What are you hiding?"

"Never mind that. Let's focus on finding the source of that smell and deal with it fast. If demons show up, we'll have trouble." Aileen can't be bothered to play along with Walt every single time, so she pushes her way into the brush, following the heady odor. Apparently, Walt and Kyle have no objections as they quickly fall in behind her.

"—Found it! This must be the place, right?" Aileen picks up a pipe from the thick grass, showing it to Walt and Kyle.

"Yes, that's definitely the source—and it's empty."

"So it's already been used, hmm? For all that, though, the lingering scent seems faint… I'd guess the concentration was weak."

Kyle nods, agreeing with Walt's theory. "It is more diluted than usual. I doubt this will draw any demons into the academy."

"Right. Then who on earth…? And why?"

"Since it's a pipe, a human was probably smoking it, don't you think? Look, there's a depression in the grass." Aileen points to a tamped-down spot that could have been left by someone sitting with their back against the tree.

"They must've dropped their pipe. Demon snuff is exhilarating if you smoke it, correct?"

"Yes. It's like a drug. If they're using it, they'll wind up a shell of themselves sooner or later. It's not the sort of thing a student could acquire on a lark… This isn't like some kid experimenting with cigarettes."

"Even if the concentration is low, there's no way that demon snuff is in circulation as a simple indulgence." Kyle says this precisely because he knows it's strictly controlled by the church.

"…And there isn't any chance that the church is spreading demon snuff around…right?" Ailey asks.

Walt shakes his head. "If they were, they wouldn't have told us to go recover it."

"I'd imagine the demon snuff you need to recover is from a source *other than* the church. What's more, I've seen a report that the church is planning to slip demon snuff into the grand prize for the swordsmanship contest, in order to expose the demon."

In response to Aileen's prediction that what happened in the game will happen again here, Kyle scowls at her. "The church would never do such a thing. If they forced a demon into its true form in the midst of a crowd of students, there would undoubtedly be victims. Depending on the concentration, demon snuff can be harmful to humans as well."

"…But if someone slipped a hefty sum to those sly foxes in the clergy, I bet they'd do it."

"Walt! You—!"

"Look, do you seriously think that the church is a perfectly righteous organization? The client who requested our current mission is the house of Mirchetta. They're completely in each other's pockets, and on top of that, it's all happening over a petty domestic squabble."

Kyle flares up, red-faced. "How dare you reveal classified secrets in front of Ailey like this!"

"Sweet Ailey probably knows all about that stuff anyway. Don't you?"

"...Well, in a way." *Through the game*, Aileen mutters to herself.

Walt looks as if he's lost interest. "At this point, what motivates the church most is a hunger for money and power. Saving humans from demons is nothing but a justification."

"There are still people in the church who don't only pay lip service to those values. At the very least, I can say with certainty the bishop is one of those people." Kyle speaks with dignity. Walt frowns, then emits a little sigh.

...I didn't expect that. Walt is actually the one who's concerned about Kyle.

Come to think of it, although the bishop had raised Kyle as a son, he'd betrayed him in the game. Conversely, she seems to recall a bad ending in which Walt betrayed the church and was killed while attempting to save Serena by none other than Kyle, who'd become an assassin.

This is the perfect chance. If I use these two to avert triggering any bad flags surrounding the swordsmanship contest...

If she plays her cards right, these two should be able to break free from their sordid futures as well.

"In that case, why don't you tell that person Kyle mentioned about the swordsmanship contest and find out the truth?"

"Yes, that's sensible. I'll contact him."

"No, I'll do it... There's no way the bishop would allow such a thing."

Kyle's expression is hard. Walt looks at him, but in the end, he says nothing. Instead, he glances at Aileen. It seems he's leaving the decision to her.

"All right, Kyle, please do that. Also, this demon snuff—would you allow me to study it a little?" If she gives it to Luc or Quartz, they may learn something useful. However, no sooner has she said it than Kyle's eyes narrow sharply, and Walt flashes a new smile that doesn't go past his lips.

"We can't have that, sweet Ailey."

"I don't know who or what you are, but you're going to give that to us."

"I only want to examine it. Please let me have it. I promise I'll report all my findings."

"You mean to the student council as well, of course."

Caught in the beam of a hand lantern, the three of them flinch guiltily, turning to look.

There are two figures by the source of the light.

"Auguste... President James..."

"S-sorry, Ailey. James is fine now, and he said he was worried about you three. I followed him, and... Um—what happened here?"

"Parenthetically, should you neglect to make that report, I will consider it a violation of the student council president's orders, and you will all be expelled. You're going to tell me absolutely everything about what it is you're doing here. None of you are simply students, are you?"

James, whose complexion is perfectly normal again, looks them over. His eyes are cold and dispassionate. Kyle's expression has gone sour. Beside him, Walt heaves a deep sigh.

"...We blew it. All right, what do we do? Would you help us out, sweet Ailey? Since you're actually a..."

"Fine. Follow me, all of you."

Stomping on Walt's foot as hard as she can, Aileen steels herself for what's about to come next.

★   ★   ★

When the members of the student council trail Aileen into the joint research lab, all Isaac says is, "Ah, I can see what happened." Luc gets to his feet, saying, "We'll need enough tea to go around," and Quartz begins setting up chairs.

They're all so very brilliant and quick on the uptake.

"So, Ailey, you're saying your group is a secret organization sent by Imperial Ellmeyer to investigate 'demon snuff,' a dangerous drug that's been circulating at Misha Academy?! Wow, that's incredible!" Auguste sums up the discussion so far, his eyes shining.

Aileen nods, smiling. "That's right. Walt and Kyle are still apprentices and active students, though. They noticed that something was off here and informed me, their superior."

"Huh? Wha—? You can't possibly be implying that you're the boss, right, my dearest Ailey!"

"Why, of course I am. Or have you and Kyle been dispatched from another, separate organiza—?"

"That's right, Auguste, sweet Ailey is our supervisor! Right, Kyle?!"

"Sure…"

Walt, who doesn't want his connection to the church to get out, immediately commits to playing along. Kyle seems to have given up. He responds in agreement, but only with the scantest of words.

They're all sitting at the largest round table in the joint research lab. Isaac, who's sitting beside Aileen, murmurs, "You've picked up more lackeys. Again. Whatever, this isn't my circus…"

"Come on, having more help is a good thing. Probably."

"...Isn't it a problem that they're all male...?"

"Huh? Come to think of it, isn't Rachel a member of your group?"

"As you know, I met her for the first time here at the academy. Besides, I don't want to get a girl involved in anything too dangerous."

"Oh, well, that's true. She is a girl..."

Auguste backs down, but Isaac, Luc, and Quartz each direct knowing looks at Aileen. Naturally, she ignores them.

"So, let me introduce you once again. He's one of the guards, so no doubt you already know him, but the fellow next to me is Isaac. Go on, say hello."

"Hi. The guy next to me is Luc, the sinister doctor. Watch what you drink; there's no telling what's in it."

"Hello. Thank you for your help." For a moment, the student council members look taken aback. Without raising his head, Luc gives a little smile. "All that's in there is something to ease your tension."

"Huh? So there seriously is something in this...?" Auguste was just about to take a sip of his black tea, but he gingerly returns the cup to its saucer instead. Everyone else follows suit.

"The glum-looking one next to him is Quartz. He's a botanist. He doesn't usually answer even when you speak to him, but he isn't ignoring you. He only talks to plants, that's all."

"......"

Wordlessly, Quartz nods to them. Isaac, who has his chin propped on his hand, continues his haphazard round of introductions. "These two are studying the composition of demon snuff. The research student bit isn't entirely for show. They're experts in their respective fields. We've also got a journalist on standby in town, ready to collect information. Then Walt and Kyle are bottom-rung odd-jobbers."

"Odd-jobbers..."

"Ha-ha. Now that's a novel title..."

Kyle and Walt mutter to themselves, looking a little wounded. However, for an off-the-cuff introduction they hadn't discussed beforehand, it's magnificent. As a matter of fact, Auguste seems to believe it completely.

"I see. Oh, did you form the guard unit partly to help with your investigation?"

"Yes, in a way. However, it's also true that I couldn't stand to see how the girls were being treated here."

"...A moment ago, you said that this 'demon snuff' makes people violent." James, who's been listening in silence the whole time, speaks up.

In order to avoid giving him too much information, she'd spoken only about the effects of demon snuff on humans. That had probably been more convenient for Walt and Kyle as well. Beside her, Walt nods. "That's right. It's thought that it makes your body tougher by affecting your state of mind."

"Could that be why girls have been treated so harshly at the academy lately?"

Aileen isn't the only one who gulps; Walt and Kyle do as well. Auguste smacks his hands together in sudden realization. "You know, I did think it had been particularly egregious lately. No one would dare to physically attack a classmate like this before."

"Now that you mention it... Yes, you're right. I had gotten it into my head that this was simply that sort of school..."

"Wait, don't tell me—does this mean demon snuff use is popular among the male students?"

"Luc, what do you think?"

When Aileen turns to him, Luc picks up the pipe that's been set in the center of the table. "I think it's very likely that they're using it without knowing it's dangerous. No doubt this evidence supports that theory."

"When you dilute the dosage, it's simply an addictive substance that makes you feel good. Basically, it's a drug. It's also possible that whoever has the connection to the source is systematically selling it off. You could make a killing with this sort of thing," Isaac suggests.

Walt gives a bitter laugh. "That sounds plausible."

"Listen, I'll help out with this. That stuff seems like bad news."

"Auguste. You're an amateur. If you poke your nose into this, you'll only make things harder for us."

Although the way Kyle puts it is harsh, what he's saying is correct. Auguste shakes his head. "I can at least ask the guys about it. Right, Ailey? That much's okay, isn't it?"

"—Yes." Aileen nods. Walt and Kyle glare at her. For professionals, not getting amateurs involved must be a cardinal rule. However, Auguste is the sort of person who'd borrow the sacred sword and become a Holy Knight. Aileen decides that, in terms of what's up ahead as well, there's no harm in asking him to help out. "Can I trust you to handle that and not behave recklessly? I'd like you to look into weird games and the sort of thing that stands out. Find out whether smoking it is popular among the boys."

"Okay. Leave it to me!"

"Ailey!"

"Is there a problem? I believe I'm your superior, aren't I, Walt?" She gives him a faint smile, and Walt *tsk*s and turns away.

Since he's attempting to use her as a cover, he'd better follow an order or two.

"Say, James, you'll help too, won't you? It's not like the student council has any reason to be less concerned about all this." Auguste turns to James, who's sitting next to him, arms folded and legs crossed.

James snorts. "Help this lot? When they're still clearly hiding something?"

"Huh...?"

"That demon snuff. You said it was dangerous to humans. Is that all?"

The perceptive question catches them off guard, and everyone goes silent.

It's only natural he'd wonder about that, though. Both now and on that earlier occasion, he'd come very close to turning into a demon. Even in the game, he'd found opym because of his sensitive demon nose.

When silence is their only answer, James narrows his eyes. Then he stands up. "I'm reporting this matter to the principal."

Everyone looks up, shocked. Aileen feels the blood drain from her face. *Oh, but at this point, if I explain myself, then just maybe...* Aileen's mind instinctively searches for a way out. Except on further thought, the only thing that comes to mind is a hellish scene of multiple volcanic eruptions, lightning strikes, and earthquakes backed by a certain man's lovely smile.

"James. This is our job. You know the principal probably has his hands full with Ashtart."

"Reporting on all serious matters and developments to the principal is the student council president's job. Or is there a reason you can't afford to have this reported?"

In response to James's cold taunt, silence falls over the group again. Walt and Kyle must want to avoid drawing the demon king's attention as much as Aileen's group does. Aside from the demon snuff, they have standing orders to kill a demon. Claude won't allow that. If they maneuver poorly, they'll end up in direct opposition to the demon king.

As if acknowledging the silence itself as an answer, James snorts and gets to his feet. "I'll go back to the dormitory, then."

"James! Listen, Ailey and the rest are doing important work. You can't expect them to not have secrets they can't freely share. You should be able to trust them anyway."

"It must be nice to be that simpleminded, Auguste—I don't trust anyone."

James makes that last remark as if he's reminding himself of where he stands, and then he finally takes his leave. Walt and Kyle exchange glances. For Nameless Priests, the end justifies the means. In fact, if they get rid of James, they'll have accomplished their mission... But...

"I'll get him to come around. The rest of you, wait here."

"Ailey."

"It would be better if we all managed to get along, wouldn't it?"

Walt and Kyle look deflated. Auguste seems relieved. Isaac and the rest wave.

Come back soon.

The moment Aileen steps out of the lab, she spots James's back. "President James! Please wait. Let's talk this—"

"...You know, come to think of it, there was something I wanted to ask you as well." James was striding away, but he suddenly stops under a streetlamp and turns around. Aileen was trotting to catch up, so she nearly runs into him. After stopping short, she backs up hastily.

"What are you?"

"Huh? I just explained—"

"Let me change the question—you saw my true form, didn't you?"

Aileen falls silent.

James tries another question, sounding bored. "If you don't want to die, answer me truthfully. Why did you keep quiet about that, and then try to cover for me?"

"……"

"Nothing to say, hmm? And you expect me to cooperate with you? Don't make me laugh. What are you trying to get me to do, now that you can hold my darkest secret over me?"

From James's sneer, she can guess at the sort of things he probably endured in the past. Evidently, even people who saved him have betrayed him in one way or another.

Aileen feels sorry for him. It's understandable he'd be wary of humans. Still… "What a pain…," she mutters.

"Huh?"

"All right, fine, I'll explain. Come out, Ribbon."

They're under a streetlamp, which means her shadow is pooling at her feet. The young fenrir pokes out of that shadow, head first. With Almond as interpreter, she'd learned that this fenrir is a little girl who loves ribbons, and so she named her Ribbon.

Ribbon is in the middle of a growth spurt, but although she's rapidly getting bigger, she's still a child. She looks at Aileen and emits a soft whine. Aileen smiles at her. "This boy says he'll play with you."

"Yip?"

"Wha—? Whoa!"

At the sight of the demon that's emerged by her feet, James freezes in place, and the delighted Ribbon lunges at him, knocking him down. Then she gambols around, energetically licking him. "Stop—stop, make this demon stop! Hey!" he shrieks.

"Listen to me, Ribbon. Remember his scent. You'd like to play tag with someone, wouldn't you?"

"Yip."

"Tag...? What in the world are you trying to do?!"

"If I'm right, President James, whoever controls the supply of demon snuff around here is trying to make you transform. I want to protect you."

James, who's been struggling under Ribbon's paws, immediately goes still. Ribbon stops licking him. She whines and tilts her head.

"Protect? What for? Why would you need to do a thing like that?"

"Why? Because if you haven't done anything bad, then isn't it only natural I feel sorry for you?"

James's eyes open very wide. Aileen calls Ribbon, then explains. "As you see, I can summon demons. I can't tell you to believe me just because of that, but... Well, if nothing else, I don't think you have to worry I might be in cahoots with the church that's hunting you."

"...If you can summon demons, I'd imagine not. Those priests are in the business of purging them."

"Besides, I'm here for Ashtart. Do you know him, President?"

At the question, James seems to flinch back. However, he quickly recovers and dons his usual sardonic smile once more.

"I have no reason to answer th— Stop that! Stop! Call off your demon!"

"Oh, don't be like that. I'm not making her do anything. Ribbon's just taken a liking to you. Haven't you, Ribbon?"

"Yip." Ribbon nods.

James has crawled away from the fenrir, putting some distance between them. Sitting awkwardly on the ground, he sighs. "The name Ashtart belongs to me."

"Huh...? No way..."

"If you think I'd bother lying now, there's something wrong with you... I'm half demon, you know." James gives a self-mocking smile, then leans back against the lamppost. "To be accurate, it was the demon name my father gave me. I discarded it a long time ago."

"...Was any of this in the original scenario?"

"The scenario?"

"Oh, um, never mind." Aileen, who's forgotten to censor herself, clears her throat and quickly moves on. "In that case, why is someone threatening to attack under that name?"

"How should I know? It's certainly not me... Although I doubt you'll simply take me at my word."

"No, I believe you. None of this would make sense otherwise." James's eyes go round again. Stroking Ribbon's head, Aileen continues. "If you were Ashtart, you'd have no reason to pick a fight with the demon king, and you'd gain nothing from distributing demon snuff. Most importantly, you wouldn't be someone who collapses from simply being near some."

The mention of his collapse seems to embarrass James. As he frowns, the crease between his eyebrows shows up so clearly in the light from the streetlamp that it's comical.

"The true culprit who is spreading demon snuff is trying to set you up. In other words, the Ashtart we're looking for is whoever's behind the demon snuff. Everything makes sense that way. A lot of things are still unclear, such as whether or not they have a connection to the church that's pursuing you, but..."

"Either way, they probably don't know I'm a demon." Ribbon sidles up to James. He strokes her head once, then abruptly looks up. "Hey, send this demon home. If anyone spots us like this, there'll be hell to pay."

"Yip?"

"And you. Don't approach me carelessly. I'm not one of you." He looks melancholy as he tells Ribbon this, and it reminds Aileen of Claude.

Is it because he's the final boss? They really do seem similar... In the game, after Claude had died and the demons were being pressed harder and harder by humans, James tried to become their new king. It seems rather obvious now that he did it mainly for the demons' sake. Since Claude is still alive and well in this world, James has no compelling reason or intent to become the demon king.

Ribbon blinks her black eyes at him, then turns around. Aileen nods. Keeping an eye on James, Ribbon slips back into the shadow, letting it swallow her.

"President James, you remind me of the one I love."

"Huh?" James looks extremely put out. "That's unpleasant. Are you saying I look like a woman?"

"Oh... W-well, there's nothing wrong with that. What I meant to say is, I'm feeling enthusiastic about this. I'll devote my entire being to protecting you, so please help me out. Don't make that report to the principal."

"I refuse."

"Come out, Ribb—"

"All right! Don't use demons as shields, you coward." James practically jumps to his feet, and he heaves a long sigh. "Very well... I'd just as rather deal with the demon king as little as possible anyway."

"Why? Does he make you want to kneel in awe or something?" The demons hold their king in very high regard.

However, James laughs dismissively. "Kneel, to a spineless man who's been fettered by a jealous woman?"

"A jea— Oh, that's, uh..." Realizing she's about to launch into an altogether unnecessary explanation about how that's a misunderstanding, she hastily shuts her mouth.

James has turned away, and the streetlamp illuminates his profile. "I may be half demon, but I do have a demon's pride. A demon king who has submitted to the Maid of the Sacred Sword is merely another human. I will not kneel to someone who is not my king."

A king is someone who responds to expectations. Aileen says no more on the matter.

For now, I'll discuss the matter of concubines with him sooner than later.

After all, being a suitable wife for him is about the only way she can help.

Before Claude has a chance to write his response, he receives another letter from his fiancée, and its subject?

Conditions for Concubines.

"How did we get onto this topic...?!" He buries his face in his hands.

Gazing out the window, where a rainstorm blusters, Keith responds casually. "She probably got the wrong idea about the young lady Serena. I'd imagine the d'Autriche family has at least a few spies embedded in the region. You were prepared for that when you decided to pay attention to her, weren't you?"

"Even if I was, why would *that* lead to *this*?!"

"She most likely wants to demonstrate her capacity as empress to tolerate you taking a woman or two on the side. Isn't that wonderful?" Keith smiles. It doesn't make Claude happy, however.

"...I understand how Cedric feels."

"Huh? And how is that?"

"It makes you want to test her. What would you have to do in order to break her or make her cry...? What, and how much, will she tolerate for your sake?"

He picks up a quill. For the moment, if she's developed some sort of misunderstanding, he should clear it up.

Worried, Keith lowers his voice. "You mustn't test her. She'll cast you aside."

"I know that... I also know she's written this because I'm making her uneasy."

"What makes you think so?"

"It's the other side of her claim that she is eminently suited to be empress."

I'll be useful to you, so please don't crush me a second time. It's probably an unconscious plea, but that's the request that lies behind Aileen's actions. The wound Cedric left is a deep one.

There's a flash, and lightning strikes outside the window.

Keith flinches, then sighs. "Milord, all in moderation. The school festival begins tomorrow. Have pity on the students."

"Yes, I'm sorry. I just saw red for a moment... I'll calm down."

"Please do. You summoned Serena again today, didn't you?"

"Yes—Almond." He snaps his fingers. A hole suddenly opens in the floor, and Almond pokes his head out.

"Deliver this letter to Aileen."

"...Demon king, are you cheating?"

"What, did Aileen say something?"

Almond's red eyes flick up and down, left and right. He seems to be trying to figure out how to respond. Claude gives a wry smile, then admonishes him gently. "You and the others are well aware of my feelings. Tell Aileen she's a naughty bride for doubting me."

"Understood! Aileen is a naughty bride!"

Scooping up the letter with his beak, Almond flies back into the hole in the floor and vanishes. After Claude snaps his fingers once more, the hole closes up.

"You've had all the demons leave the town, correct?"

"Yes. Beelzebuth will return as soon as he's sent all the nearby demons farther away."

"I think Bel will be able to endure it, but... Don't let any other demons near the city. That smell will make them lose their heads. I'd like to do something about the ones who aren't responding to my call, too, but..."

"I'll go around town with Beelzebuth and conduct a careful search, starting tomorrow. We'll do all we can. It would be better if you stayed here, Master Claude, since there's Ashtart to deal with."

"True, but I'd prefer not to. It's too confining on more than one level. I'd really rather—"

Suddenly, Claude blinks. Keith's glasses gleam. "Master Claude. Were you perhaps thinking of going to amuse yourself at the school festival just now?"

His attendant's instincts are sharp. Claude averts his eyes. However, Keith knows him well, and he promptly gets right in his face and threatens him. "Milord. You are naive, and every time you slipped out of the abandoned castle and went to have fun in the capital, you caused trouble wherever you went. Have you forgotten how hard I had to work to clean up the messes you left behind?"

"You know I haven't caused any problems lately."

"Just you try going off to play at the festival when other people are working. I'll tell Lady Aileen how you were very nearly sold off to a brothel."

Claude grimaces. After reminding him one more time that he's expected to stay at the palace, Keith piles a veritable mountain of documents on Claude's desk for good measure.

However, his feelings are honest. The brilliant idea that has begun to grow inside him makes the rainstorm stop, and patches of blue appear above.

A balloon a child has lost drifts into the cloudless sky.

On the first day of the festival, with the academy already bustling with all sorts of people, a duck dashes through the school grounds. "I'm with the guards! The thing you just hid behind your back is against school regulations! I'm confiscating it!"

"?! C'mon, it's the school festival, gimme a brea— Waugh!"

The student who's trying to argue with Aileen staggers as something yanks him back by the shoulder. "Hurry up and take it out," a second duck says, threatening him from behind. The student nods earnestly, then brings out the item.

"The guard unit... Wh-why are they ducks?"

"I saw another one over there. It sounds like there are five; somebody counted them."

During that whispered conversation, she inspects the confiscated item. It doesn't appear to be demon snuff. "All right, let's move on, Jame— I mean, Blue."

"Why do I have to wear this...?"

"Oh, there you are, Ai— I mean Red and Blue!"

A third duck approaches, waving its wing vigorously and calling out their code names. However, a child it passes intercepts the duck before it reaches the group. Isaac slips past the occupied pair and smoothly joins the others.

"How's it look over there, President Duck? Oh, wait, you're Blue right now."

"Do you have a death wish?"

"Curse your own luck of the draw before you resent me. Boy am I glad there were only five costumes."

"—Why are we wearing these in the first place, Ailey Calois?!" James sounds indignant.

Aileen answers with a straight face. "Call me Red. And it's because if we're dressed like this, we'll catch people by surprise."

It isn't a total lie. Although her personal reason is that she doesn't know when Claude may turn up and where.

Master Claude had that duck on his mind. That means we'll just have to increase the number of ducks. And that's how it came to this.

The third duck waves bye-bye to the child, then walks up to them. "These are a huge hit. It's awkward that the only way to tell each other apart is the color of the ribbons on our chests, though. Also, I'm not happy about the fact that I'm Pink. I wanted to be Red."

Auguste fiddles with the pink ribbon on his fluffy chest. James, whose ribbon is blue, turns on Isaac again. "You were a founding member of the guard unit, weren't you?!"

"We don't discriminate like that. We're all fellow lackeys, so let's get along."

"Who's a lackey?"

"Okay, okay. Report from Black and Yellow: all's well on their end as well."

As an aside, Black is Kyle and Yellow is Walt. Their eyes seemed dead and vacant when they started their shift, but apparently they're doing their jobs properly at least.

"Rachel was asking what we were going to do for our lunch breaks."

"Whoa! Is it that late already?! I have to go put my name down for the swordsmanship contest!"

"In that case, let's go look around the contest venue. Isaac, tell Black and Yellow they can go ahead and take lunch."

"Roger that."

After parting with Isaac, she, James, and Auguste head over to the venue for the swordsmanship contest. Up ahead, they can see a round arena surrounded by a high wall. It's apparently a very old building that's been there longer than the school itself, and it's only opened once a year, on this day.

"Aren't you going to compete in the swordsmanship contest, Blue?"

"Don't call me Blue. I wouldn't go in for a thing like that. It's just a hassle."

"Walt and Kyle say they aren't entering, either. It'll be lonesome all on my own."

Auguste looks unhappy, but Aileen would really rather not have James get involved with the contest if at all possible.

Thanks to the man Kyle simply refers to as the bishop, it sounds as though the grand prize has been changed to something that has no connection to demon snuff. However, the church isn't so lackadaisical that she can just take them at their word. Besides, Aileen knows for a fact that Kyle is betrayed by the bishop he respects according to the game's plot. More than anything, Aileen has personally seen for herself that the game's events generally still occur even if their shape has changed slightly.

"I'll cheer you on enough for the rest of them, Auguste."

"In that case, I suppose I should give it my best. Ah, I'll go register."

The arena's entrance is still closed, but there are stalls lined up around it, and a feverish excitement is in the air. The competition is fought with mock swords so that no one will get hurt, but it isn't just for students. In classic school festival style, even outsiders are allowed to compete. Because the top three contestants are awarded modest cash prizes, there are quite a few adults who come to test their mettle. As a result, in the shadows, some people are preparing to place bets on the outcome, but Aileen decides to overlook it while on patrol.

"Looks like there's quite a few contenders. Do you think Auguste will manage to win?"

"That muscle-head should be fine."

Aileen thinks that's an awful way to put it, but James sounds convinced. He acknowledges Auguste's strength, if nothing else.

True, even in the game, Auguste won, but…

There are some knights who are clearly not students among the contestants. If he's able to fight on equal terms with them when he's still in school, his obvious skill will cement his future career as a Holy Knight.

"I've never seen Auguste fight. I'm looking forward to it. The executive committee is running the festival, and the only thing on our schedule is patrolling as guards for the event, correct?"

"Right. Serena said that the demon king is terribly busy, though, and there's no telling when he'll be able to come. We shouldn't let our security lapse."

Come to think of it, Claude had said that things were going to be busy in the letter he'd sent her the other day. *Almond called me a naughty bride or something like that… I wonder what that meant.*

Auguste has removed his duck head in order to register. As she watches him from a distance, she thinks, perplexed: What has she done that's naughty? She's confirmed that Claude has summoned Serena multiple times. She'd just assumed he intended to make her his local mistress, but—*I need no concubines. All I want is you.* That response had made her heart flutter a bit.

"If the demon king isn't coming, we really will have to be on the alert."

"I think relying on the demon king is a mistake in the first place."

"Oh good. Are you still accepting entries?"

At the sound of that voice, Aileen freezes up. Next to her, James has dexterously managed to fold his arms despite the limitations of his duck costume, but he stops moving as well.

The person who called out comes to a sudden stop just as he's walking by Aileen and James.

Glossy black hair. A tall, slender build. His most striking feature is the silver mask covering the top half of his face. People aren't involuntarily turning back to look at him because he's ugly, though. One can tell he's beautiful simply from the contours of his half-hidden face— Or actually, the very fact that it is hidden only heightens his allure and beauty.

As if he's drowned in that beauty, James gasps. "De...de, de..."

"...There are more ducks now."

His murmur sounds impressed. Aileen has been on the verge of fleeing reality, but that offhand comment brings her to her senses.

M-Master Claude?!

"Thanks for waiting— Huh? Principal...?"

Auguste has come back, holding his duck's head. His mouth is hanging open in complete dumbfounded surprise. When he hears that remark, the masked man's lips tense up.

"I'm not the principal."

"Huh? Th-then you're the demon king, aren't you?"

"True, I am disguised as the demon king, but I'm not him. I'm a passing traveler. An ordinary person and no more."

What is he even talking about?

He may say he's "disguised," but he's only wearing a mask and simpler clothes. The token attempt at a mask has only doubled his charms, and it isn't hiding anything. In the first place, the demon king disguised as the demon king is still just the demon king.

Auguste isn't sure how to respond to this claim, but then he looks up with a gasp. "Oh! Are you disguised as someone ordinary as part of the security detail?"

"...I see. That's what I can tell Keith. Let's go with that, then."

"Don't mock us! As if that excuse would ever fly when you look like that!" The temperature of James's voice has dropped below absolute zero. He glares at Claude. In his right hand, Claude is holding a packet of fish-and-chips, while his left arm is hugging a large stuffed cat. He won a prize somewhere along the way. Claude is quite obviously enjoying the festival. However, his shapely eyebrows draw together in a gentle frown in response to the outcry. "Even the demon king carries his own belongings."

"That's not what I'm talking about!"

She can tell what little loyalty James had has plummeted straight to rock bottom and embedded itself there with a crash.

"Still, no one pointed it out before now. You're sharp."

"...I think they were probably just too scared to say anything..."

"Really? In the capital, I went around without a mask, and even then, no one caught on."

Apparently he goes out incognito, or thinks he does, to have fun in the capital as well. The demon king lives a surprisingly unrestrained life.

"By the way, you're with the student council, aren't you? Are duck costumes the council uniform or something?"

"Oh! ...S-something like that, yes... Mm-hmm."

"Don't they make it difficult to move? I doubt they're suitable for security work. You'll be eye-catching and far too conspicuous."

His concern is completely legitimate, but Claude is clearly more eye-catching and conspicuous. Auguste, the only one whose face is showing, responds with a tense, diplomatic smile. "I-it is the school festival, so... These are just like your demon king disguise, Principal!"

"Ah. I see. I'm sorry; there's much about the world I have yet to learn. Keith's warned me on that count as well... Is there a rule that the principal must not attend the festival?"

"N-noooo, nothing like that, but..."

"You may speak freely. It's only natural for the demon king to be unwelcome." Like a condemned criminal, Claude softly lowers his long eyelashes.

That gesture stirs up every protective instinct to incredible effect. Even the people around them, who'd been watching the scene unfold with bated breath, instantly begin murmuring to each other. It's human nature to want to protect beautiful things and keep them from breaking. That's true regardless of gender or background.

Apparently, Auguste's spirit of chivalry has been thoroughly aroused; he speaks up hastily. "N-no, nothing of the sort. As far as the principal is concerned, it's technically work! Right, James?!"

"That's, erm, well... If there's something that requires your attention here, it's only sensible to be concerned about it, I suppose..."

"I see. In that case, first and foremost, I'd like you to tell me how to enter the swordsmanship contest."

"Oh, I can explain; I just did it myself. I also know of some stalls with incredibly delicious menu items," Auguste chimes in.

"N-never mind that, registering comes first. There's no time."

Claude has captured two pawns with ease, and a shudder runs down Aileen's spine. *So age and gender have nothing to do with it?! Was this man simply born to be worshipped?! He's dangerous beyond belief. I must get Master Keith to take him home and quickly! Nothing good can come of this!*

Aileen sidles back furtively, so Claude won't notice—and then their eyes meet.

He's watching her. Very, very intently.

"......"

"You're...the duck who came to get my seal, aren't you?"

She jerks her head up and down, nodding emphatically. She's hoping to end the conversation there. However, Claude has closed the distance between them before she's aware of it, and his face is right in front of the duck's head.

"...It's very odd. I'm incredibly curious about you. Why don't you ever speak?"

From behind the mask, those red eyes are scrutinizing her. His ferocious gaze seems to be exploring her entire body, attempting to expose everything within eyeshot. His dangerous, enticing aura makes her skin prickle, and she breaks out in goose bumps all over. Screaming inwardly, she retreats, but her back comes up against a wall. When she twists, trying to change directions, Claude thrusts his hand out and blocks her way.

Pinning a duck to the wall! What an unsatisfying visual!! Why couldn't he do this when she was Aileen? She shakes her head, objecting desperately— *Not like this!*

"Why do you run from me? I'd like to talk to you."

His thin lips curve into a smile, but his tone is cold. Even so, her whole body feels deliciously numb, and she can't budge.

"Would you show me your face?"

"E-excuse me... They're about to close registration for the contest," Auguste calls from a distance. Claude's fingers are reaching for the duck's head, but then he stops. Sighing in resignation, he turns on his heel.

Still leaning against the wall, Aileen weakly slides down into a crouch. Belatedly, she notices her heart pounding. That was a close call.

Wh-what intense sex appeal... Is it possible that Master Claude has been holding back with me? Aghhh...

Technically, fear would have been the expected response. While her heart had skipped a beat, it wasn't because she was scared. She tries to rub her red cheeks, then realizes that isn't possible in the duck costume.

When she looks up, Claude has already finished registering for the swordsmanship contest, and Auguste and James seem to be leading him somewhere else. The freewheeling demon king has no idea what she's feeling.

But... Perhaps it's all right. Just for a little while.

He resolved to live as the demon king at a very early age, and he hasn't been blessed with many typical human experiences. It's

important for him to have those as well if he's going to become emperor one day. On that thought, she silently watches his back disappear into the crowd. Under different circumstances, she would have been able to go with him.

"Ailey! Bad news!"

"Wh-what now?!"

She's been so preoccupied feeling like a smitten young maiden, she completely overreacts to Walt and Kyle when they call out to her. However, neither of them takes so much as a step back. They aren't wearing their duck costumes, and their faces are serious. "We've got trouble. Instead of the grand prize, it sounds as though they've put demon snuff in the arena itself."

"...What do you mean?"

Aileen gives them a dubious look, and Kyle bites his lip. "The bishop told me it was all he could do to keep them from tampering with the prize."

"A likely story! If they're going to spike something with demon snuff, it's the same whether they put it in the prize or in the arena. When he said he'd stop them, he was lying. The whole church is in on this. How long are you planning to believe this bishop of yours?" Walt asks him, spitting out the words.

When Kyle responds, it sounds as if he's making excuses. "I'm told the demon snuff they used isn't very potent. It shouldn't affect the students. The most it will do is hurt the demon who's concealing itself, and—"

"...I'd expected the church's betrayal...but that isn't the problem now!" Aileen mutters hollowly.

"What's the matter?" Walt asks.

"The principal is competing in the swordsmanship contest. If he transforms into a demon—!"

Walt and Kyle turn pale.

There is someone who can stop him. Aileen has the sacred sword. However, that will mean revealing her presence to Claude, and as soon as that happens, it's Game Over. He may force her to leave, before she's learned the threatening Ashtart's true identity or anything at all.

In the first place, if Claude turns into a dragon, there's no guarantee that Mirchetta will make it through in one piece. A single ray from his mouth could turn the surrounding area into a blasted wasteland.

"I'll think of a way to stop the demon king. For now, you two contact the church!"

"A-all right."

She has to do something. Besides, overcoming this situation will prove beyond a doubt she's worthy to be the demon king's wife.

"...So think of a way to get Master Claude to peacefully withdraw from the swordsmanship contest immediately!" Arms crossed, Aileen issues orders to the usual group.

Since Claude is wandering around the school festival, they've ended up crowded into the guard room, and they all look rather unhappy.

"As if that's even possible? It's weird that he's participating in the first place. There's no way that's going to be any kind of contest. Where's the fun in that, Demon King?"

"I hear he's given himself handicaps—no using magic, no fighting with his dominant hand—and he still cleared the preliminaries." Jasper reveals information absolutely nobody wants to hear.

Luc gives a weak laugh. "He's enjoying this to the fullest, isn't he...?"

"...Aren't the other contestants angry? I hope he isn't making enemies for himself." Although you wouldn't expect it from his devilish appearance, Quartz is kind.

Aileen sighs as well. "Master Claude is skilled with both the pen and the sword, and beautiful besides. People will be jealous; there's really no way around it."

"Hey, no one asked to hear about how great lover boy out there is."

"I'm only stating the facts. I've left dealing with the church to Walt and Kyle. Like Claude, Auguste is participating in the swordsmanship contest, and I've foisted all the odd jobs from both the guard unit and the student council onto President James to make sure he'll be nowhere near the arena."

"The poor president. This isn't his mess, but he's certainly paying for it..."

"I've asked Rachel to help him out. He'll be all right. He's brilliant, after all." No one argued with Aileen on that point. "That means we'll just have to do something about Master Claude on our own."

"Under these circumstances when we can't afford to let him see any of us? You're serious?"

"Yes. You can put pressure on the church, can't you, Jasper?"

"I did lob a rock at them, but I dunno if it'll make it in time."

"That's all right. If they hear that the demon king is taking part in the contest, the church may panic and order Walt and Kyle to round up the demon snuff in circulation. If the church's demon snuff vanishes from Misha Academy, it'll simplify matters later on. I'm all for it."

In the first place, as an organization that kills demons, the church is an obstacle to most of their plans. Aileen would prefer it if they were out of the picture entirely, James included. The sooner the better.

"No matter how unlikely it may be, though, I want to avoid any situation that might turn Master Claude into a demon. We know a trap using demon snuff has been set at the arena, so we'll have to get him away from there." Oblivious to her feelings, the illustrious demon king is hurtling down the road toward the championship.

Isaac rests his chin in his hands. "Well, it sounds like he's handicapping himself quite a bit. There's always a chance he might just flat-out lose during the final match."

"You know my Master Claude would never lose! Be serious about this."

"...Aileen. As Isaac pointed earlier, you're just bragging at this point," Quartz points out calmly. Aileen frowns. However, everyone is looking at her, and they all seem to agree with Quartz, so she clears her throat.

With an awkward smile, Jasper raises his hand and changes the subject. "What about having someone who can last until the finals set a trap for him?"

"It won't work. Auguste was thrilled about getting to fight the demon king, and he wants a fair match. Besides, we can't allow the existence of demon snuff to become public knowledge."

"In that case, all we can rely on are those two upperclassmen, huh? Except there's no way even those two could beat the demon king."

"...If no one minds, I have a suggestion."

"What is it, Luc?"

"Let's dose the demon king with a potion and put him to sleep. I thought something like this might happen, so I've been developing a formula that's sure to work, even on the demon king or a dragon." Luc says this frightening idea with a breezy smile, and the room goes dead silent.

Glancing down and away, Isaac mutters. "You thought something like this might happen? What sort of situations have you been thinking about as you putter away in your lab, you mad scientist?"

"Luc... That potion isn't finished yet."

"I guarantee its effectiveness. The swordsmanship contest will end before the demon king even wakes. Isn't that the ideal scenario?"

Jasper frowns. "Didn't Quartz just say it wasn't finished?"

"That's because there are still individual differences to account for when gauging whether or not a potion will work. In that sense, it isn't finished yet."

"I get the impression that wasn't what he meant..."

"It won't pose a danger to Master Claude?"

"Not at all. It's certain to put him to sleep, nothing more." As Luc speaks, he looks Aileen in the eye.

Jasper murmurs to Quartz, "Not...forever, right...?"

"According to our preliminary calculations, the effects should last for about three hours. There will be no lingering drowsiness. After he wakes, he'll feel rested, his circulation will be improved, and all the stiffness will be gone from his shoulders. It will also ease eye fatigue. It isn't bitter either. Any solution it's mixed with will taste sweet, mellow, and be easy to drink. Mixing it with soil renders it harmless."

"What?! That sounds fantastic. Heck, I'd like some of that for me ol' bones."

"Unfortunately, it's certain to kill anyone who isn't the demon king. It's specially designed to work on him alone, so I don't recommend trying it."

"That's some dangerous medicine! What kind of freaky stuff are you two developing?"

"What's your call, Aileen? They say it's lethal for anybody who's not the demon king, but safe for him."

"That's fine, then. If we have him sleep for a little while and forfeit the match, it will count as a loss and keep him away from the rest of the tournament." She does feel a bit sorry for him, but they have no choice. If Claude sounds depressed in his next letter, she'll cheer him up. She could even write a few of those embarrassing things for his sake.

"And, Jasper? One more thing: Please find a way to inform Master Keith of the current situation. We can rely on him to retrieve Master Claude. However, take care not to give away our presence here."

"Sure thing. Still, not being able to use the demons is pretty inconvenient."

"There's no way around that. I'm told Master Claude has ordered all the demons to distance themselves from the town."

She'd heard as much from Almond. Once the coast was clear, Aileen had immediately tried to summon him, but he'd only poked his head out of her shadow to explain where things currently stood. According to him, Claude had given them strict orders not to set foot in town... So, Almond had said, while it was all right to show his head, he couldn't bring his feet out. She'd found this bit of logic rather charming. Setting that aside, though...

Master Claude may have noticed the demon snuff. And yet... Is he trying to deal with it on his own?

What a troublesome man. She can't simply stand by and watch this.

"Anyway, how are we going to slip it to him?"

"Oh, that's easy. Master Claude is never on guard against poison," Aileen says. She already has a plan.

"I've brought you a drink," Rachel says, holding a pitcher of water out to Claude. Swallowing hard, Aileen watches through a crack in the door.

For some reason, although there's no sign who authorized it and got it ready for him, Claude has a special dressing room all to himself. In that room, he accepts the pitcher—and the dose of sleep medicine mixed into its contents—without a trace of suspicion. Rachel takes the initiative and pours him a cup, and he doesn't seem to question that either. Typical behavior for a member of the imperial family, who's grown up feeling it's only natural to have people wait on him.

"It's excellent water drawn from the wells in this area."

"How quaint. In that case, I would love some." Lifting the cup to his lips, Claude drinks.

It was like this when he ate the aphrodisiac-laced cookies Aileen had given him, too. Claude isn't concerned about being poisoned. His body is human, but he's built up a tolerance for poisons. In addition, his magic neutralizes them. His mindset regarding poisons is paradoxical. Since they don't work on him, there's no need to be on his guard against them.

That means the only problem here is whether or not Luc and Quartz's potion will work on him.

No changes are apparent after he finishes the first glass of water. Rachel kindly pours him a second glass, then retires from the room. She doesn't close the door all the way. Once in the corridor, she murmurs to Aileen, "Um, will that do...?"

"Yes, that's enough. Thank you, Rachel. Pour that water out on the ground at once."

"All right. Be careful, Master Ailey."

After watching until Rachel's disappeared down the hall, she peeks into the room again. Claude has finished the second glass, and as he stands up, he mutters to himself, "Maybe I'll take a breather for a bit..."

It looks as if he's begun to feel drowsy. Claude lies down on the simple bed in the corner of the room. Aileen doesn't even want to think about why a dressing room would be this well furnished.

What's important is whether the potion has worked or not. Almost immediately, she hears the rhythm of his breathing slow. He's asleep.

Perfect. Still in her duck costume, Aileen strikes a victory pose, then softly closes the door. *Master Claude's next match is the finals, an hour from now. If he stays knocked out until then, our problems are solved!*

Just in case, she moves farther down the hall and takes a seat. She'll be able to keep an eye on the door to Claude's dressing room from there. It might be slightly boring for an hour, but strangely, the idea that she's guarding Claude's slumber makes her smile a little.

Now that the moment of tension has passed, a yawn escapes Aileen. Come to think of it, it's no surprise she's tired after all the running around. *President James shouldn't have the time to come anywhere near here. Walt and Kyle will retrieve the demon snuff... Is there anything I've overlooked...?*

If the swordsmanship contest ends without incident, the events that led to James transforming into the final boss will all have been averted.

In the game, the closing ball directly follows the tournament, but the only thing to worry about there is the condemnation of the villainess. Rachel doesn't seem to have any interest in becoming Princess Lily White at this point, and as long as they remain vigilant, everything will probably be fine on that front.

In that case, Serena will be Princess Lily White. She said she'd win the contest and pick Master Claude as her dance partner...even though he already has a fiancée. She's got a lot of nerve. Given that she's currently Ailey and not Aileen, there isn't a lot she can do about it. Drowsiness keeps creeping up on her, and she can't seem to get her thoughts in order. *I don't want her to dance with Master Claude, though.* Just as she thinks that, she hears a voice.

"Master Claude, it's nearly time. I've come to fetch you."

"—Serena. I'm not Claude right now. I'm just Claw, an ordinary person."

Who in the world came up with that character? The bizarre name wakes her up instantly. *Wait, what?! It's already time—and Master Claude is awake! Why didn't the potion work?!* Her eyes go to the dressing room door. Claude emerges, wearing his mask and sword.

Serena gazes at him, cheeks flushed. "Heh-heh. Oh yes, I remember now. Did you eat the cookies I made?"

"Yes."

"...Um, how do you feel?" Serena gives Claude a searching look. She's observing him, just as Aileen does. When she registers that, something clicks.

Th-that woman! Did she dose Master Claude with an aphrodisiac— No! Don't tell me it interacted with our potion!! What did she try to do to Claude? And how is she going to make up for ruining their plan? The confusion and anger make Aileen want to lunge at her with a flying kick and haul her up by her shirtfront, but Claude's next remark blunts her enthusiasm.

"Quite pleasant. You didn't try anything untoward with those cookies, did you?"

"N-no, of course not. If you're well, I-I'm glad."

Claude nods coolly, then sets off. Serena follows him, looking oddly chagrined.

Th-that was close... He was definitely keeping a close eye on Serena's reaction just now—but this is no time to feel relieved! What's happened to the demon snuff?!

Aileen's supposed to meet with Walt and Kyle before Claude's match begins in order to get on the same page. She rushes to their rendezvous point, going in the opposite direction from the one Claude took. However, partway there, she encounters two ducks running down the corridor. They're out of breath, and she's instantly sure things aren't going according to plan. Their yellow and black ribbons confirm it's Walt and Kyle.

"Ailey, the demon king is awake! We saw him waiting his turn! What happened?!"

"Didn't the medicine work?"

"I thought it had, but maybe it didn't... H-how did it go on your end?!"

"When the bishop learned that the demon king is here, he confessed everything." Kyle's voice is stiff. Whatever happened, it couldn't have been good. "The client pressured them to kill the demon that's hiding here as soon as possible. They said it won't matter even if there are a few victims among the bystanders, so the church prepared some fairly potent demon snuff. It wouldn't be strange if the demon king really does fully transform. The bishop said he was blinded by the money and accepted the request...!"

"Kyle, that can come later. More importantly, the demon snuff's been set up in some really awkward spots. There are four stone lanterns that are scheduled to be lit when the final match begins, one in each corner of the arena. All of them have some. Once they're lit, it won't take long before the air is full of exactly what we don't want. Those lanterns are heavy, and moving them would take time. More than anything, church hands are watching the arena, meaning it won't be possible to do anything on the sly."

"Hang on. Aren't the finals scheduled to start any minute now?!"

"Yes. Auguste and the demon king are about to have their match."

In other words, Claude is headed to that very spot even as they speak.

"Also, the church has given us an additional order. We're supposed to directly use demon snuff on the demon king."

"What?!"

"Under the circumstances, I'll give it to you straight—our client is the son of Duke Mirchetta. Apparently, he wants to drive away the regent, namely the demon king. He's made an additional request to the church and sent a pile of money along with it. It should be obvious by now that the church accepted. Even if he is the crown prince, if he turns into a demon, they'll have an excuse to kill him."

What appalling logic. Aileen nearly groans.

"When our handlers heard our report, instead of getting flustered, they turned around and outright said it was a great opportunity. Duke Mirchetta's son is even preparing to send soldiers to kill the demon king once he's transformed. It must be nice to be that unconcerned. The common folk are the only ones who are going to get dragged into this, after all. We'll die, and it won't mean a thing."

"We have our orders, though, so we have to fight the demon king. We can't remove the demon snuff, either. If we refuse to obey, the church will declare us traitors and send assassins after us. Why did I ever go through all that training and become a Nameless Priest...?!"

"It was so you could protect people, yes? I won't let them use you two for anything else."

Kyle's fists are trembling, and Walt's wearing a scornful smile, but when Aileen speaks, they both look at her. She draws a deep breath, putting her thoughts in order.

Aileen can't remove the lanterns and demon snuff on her own. The church, which is running the tournament, wouldn't let her do it anyway. If she tries to remove them by force, she'll end up openly clashing with the church and drawing attention to herself. If she makes Walt and Kyle do anything that goes against their orders, it's sure to steer them toward the bad ending where they're killed by the church's hunters. How can she stop Claude while preventing all of that from happening?

And how can she foil this ridiculous plan to turn Claude into a demon and kill him?

"—Very well. Let's give the church what it wants and have you fight the demon king."

"Huh?"

Then they can just bow down before his might.

The surprisingly functional duck costume has openings in the tips of its wings, which allows Aileen to hold a sword.

The long corridor she's in seems like a tunnel that goes on forever. Aileen stands there, her back to the light. The arena lies just beyond it.

Even as a human, Master Claude is strong. I'll simply have to force everyone else to bear witness to that strength.

That way, no one will even dream of turning him into a demon ever again.

Slow footsteps echo from the depths of the corridor. Claude is coming. Aileen draws a deep breath, getting a better grip on her sword.

Claude has a sword bound to his left hand with a strip of cloth. When he notices who's barring his way, he blinks. "…Is that you again, duck? What is it this time?"

Aileen bites her lip, bracing herself before she starts flipping through the papers she's prepared.

Demon King.

"As I said, I'm not the demon king right now."

Your fiancée is not a decent woman.

Claude shuts his mouth. His eyes skim over the words on the pages Aileen keeps turning.

BECOMING ENGAGED TO TWO BROTHERS LIKE THAT IS PROOF OF HER UNSEEMLY WAYS.

I'D WAGER SHE'S DECEIVING YOU AS WELL. YOU SHOULD RID YOURSELF OF HER.

YOU LEFT HER BEHIND IN THE CAPITAL BECAUSE SHE WAS NOTHING MORE THAN A BOTHER, CORRECT?

Her first fiancé hadn't loved her. It would be completely understandable if someone with that sort of experience doubts her second fiancé.

PRINCE CEDRIC CAST HER ASIDE. THAT SHOULD TELL YOU WHAT SHE'S WORTH.

However, Aileen doesn't doubt Claude. After all, she's well aware that she is loved.

A sudden explosion rings out. The audience cheers, mistakenly thinking the final match has begun. For some reason, however, the figure that appears out of the smoke is a duck, but the one who follows it is the masked warrior Claw—or rather, the man everyone knows is the demon king and current principal of the academy.

"I did think you were an oddly intriguing duck. You're rather remarkable."

The sheaf of papers Aileen had been holding is impaled on the tip of Claude's sword. He shakes them off, then turns to face her again. Aileen had just barely managed to evade that first attack. Sweat trickles down her temples. *I—I was trying to anger him just a little, but...*

"You've insulted my fiancée. Surely you knew an apology wouldn't be enough to save you, yes?"

Her little stunt has incurred far more wrath than she bargained for.

Claude charges again. She blocks his sword squarely, but he forces her to give ground. Desperately, she just manages to hold him in check. Below his mask, Claude is smiling. "There isn't much force behind your sword. I'm not even sure whether you're a man or a woman— Who are you?"

"......!"

"Oh, you don't have to tell me. I'll have my answer as soon as I cut that costume to ribbons." He sounds happy, but it's all Aileen can do not to shriek. He swings at her again, this time from the side. When she dodges, he cuts the first stone lantern down, just as she'd intended.

G-good... All according to plan!

There is one person who can destroy the lanterns and rampage without spawning a complaint or arousing the suspicion of the church or anyone else—Claude himself. Not only that, but this is a sword fighting contest held in an arena. A little property damage can be explained away as just another part of the show.

If Aileen and her people can't demolish the lanterns, that simply meant Claude would have to do it. And...

"This won't be much of a match if all you do is run away. What are you trying to—?"

In his dogged pursuit of Aileen, Claude has destroyed a second lantern, but then he suddenly leaps backward. Another duck is already lying in wait for him there. Smoothly evading its attack, he laughs. "Three against one, hmm? I can't fathom why you came as ducks."

With Walt and Kyle joining the battle under these circumstances, *it will obviously be in order to protect the demon snuff lanterns.* This natural interpretation of their appearance means they won't have to fear being accused of betraying the church.

Under the illusion they're watching some sort of grand performance, the audience roars.

Walt attacks Claude from behind, swinging his blade down toward his back, and Claude parries. The third lantern crashes to the ground, crumbling. Just one more to go.

"Ailey, someone from the church is trying to light that last lantern!"

"Where do you think you're looking?"

Right as Aileen turns around, Claude's blade slices the air right above her head. He's only using a sword, but a blast of wind erupts, and the person who was trying to approach the stone lantern goes flying.

"What are you after? Did you have some ulterior purpose for insulting Aileen?"

"I hope you haven't forgotten about us!"

Walt launches a sudden attack, forcing Claude to whirl around. When Kyle drives his sword forward with a thrust, they're treated to a display of positively inhuman swordplay. Against two opponents, even Claude is hard-pressed and he concedes some ground.

"Huh…? Wha-what is happening?!"

Auguste heard the commotion and has finally come out to see what's going on. Kyle promptly yells at him.

"Auguste, help us out!"

"W-with what?"

"Say it as loud as you can! Stuff like how the demon king's fiancée is ugly!"

"Even if that's true, isn't that something you're never supposed to say?!"

Claude's bloodlust skyrockets. Turning aside all of Walt's swift strikes, he knocks back Kyle's heavy blows as well. Then he aims a merciless stream of attacks at Aileen, who has her back to that last lantern. The lantern cracks loudly, splitting right in two, along with her—or that's what would have happened if the blade hadn't stopped.

"……"

"A-Ailey, are you okay?!"

Aileen has crouched down. Right above her head, Auguste has caught Claude's attack. Then, using both hands, he pushes his opponent's sword back, knocking it away. Putting some distance between them, Claude looks at his own hand, then at Auguste, startled. Auguste straightens up, gazing around.

"What in the world? The arena's falling to pieces, and there're people sprawled out on the ground—"

The lanterns are practically rubble. The referees and other staff who should have been overseeing the match—in other words, the church's agents—have been sent flying by Claude, and they're all unconscious.

"Auguste. To tell you the truth, this is a show that's supposed to precede the final match. The point is to display the might of the newly formed guard."

"A show? Nobody told me about that."

"We thought we'd surprise you." Walt and Kyle start trying to put Auguste and Claude off the scent.

"Our apologies to you as well, Principal. That did get pretty exciting, though, didn't it?"

"…You're telling me you called my fiancée ugly for the sake of a mere performance?" Claude's voice is icy cold, and everyone freezes up. Walt's lips start to move, saying, "No, but I mean, that portrait…," but apparently he doesn't have the courage to say it loudly enough for Claude to hear.

"That duck insulted my fiancée. I won't be satisfied until I cut it to pieces."

"My dear Ailey... The demon king is incredibly angry. What did you say?"

She had no idea he'd get this mad—well, no, that's actually not true.

"In the first place, if you're apologizing, I don't think you should be wearing those duck heads while you do it."

"Oh, that's a good point." Walt obediently removes the head of his costume, and Kyle follows suit.

"We've been terribly rude in the service of our own convenience. Please don't be angry with us."

Not good. This development is categorically not good. Inside her costume, Aileen is dripping with greasy sweat. She has to make a run for it somehow—but she doubts Claude will let that happen.

Auguste drops a hand onto her shoulder. "Come on, Ailey, you take yours off, too, and apolo—"

"What the hell do you think you're doing, my foolish master?!"

Immediately following that cry, an attack with lethal intent behind it falls out of the sky, heading straight for Claude. He casually dodges it, then frowns. "...Keith...you're back already."

"Goooood day, milord. A little bird told me a certain someone was out and about enjoying themselves, so I asked Bel to fly me back on the double."

His lips are smiling, but Keith's eyes are pure danger. Beelzebuth touches down a few moments later, then kneels at Claude's feet. "Sire. I've carried out all your orders, and so I have returned."

"I see. You went and got it all done, hmm...?"

"You look disappointed, Master Claude! Did you have fun at the school festival?! What is this mess? It's absolutely your fault, that's what it is! What did you do this time?!"

"I'm the one who broke most of it, but it wasn't my fault."

"As if anyone's going to accept an excuse like that?!" At Keith's scream, Aileen starts to feel a little guilty. Practically speaking, the only way to neatly conclude this incident is by saying Claude went wild. And of course, Aileen is the one who made that happen.

However, Claude isn't privy to these details, and he speaks impassively. "You don't have to get so worked up. I brought souvenirs for you both. You're looking forward to that, aren't you, Bel."

"Of course, my king."

"Boy oh boy, I sure am, too! Whatever could it be, hmm?!"

"Your souvenirs are the church hands who are lying on the ground over there."

Keith's expression changes dramatically. Walt and Kyle's cheeks tense up ever so slightly. Only Claude seems unchanged. It's as if what he's saying isn't the least bit important. "They set some sort of trap in the stone lanterns. Retrieve it and investigate. Browbeat the church. They're hiding something."

"...Ahh, I see. It was one of those things..."

"I genuinely was working. Now you have nothing to complain about, correct?"

Claude smiles thinly. Aileen is stunned.

S-so he really had noticed the demon snuff? When?! In that case, why did I go through all this?

Keith sighs. "Master Claude... You aren't fooling me. The main reason you came was the school festival, and this was simply coincidence, wasn't it?"

"No, that's not..."

"I'll tell Lady Aileen on you. About all the you-know-what in your past."

Claude's eyebrows rise in dismay. What could it be? Aileen waits impatiently for revelatory details. However, Keith already seems satisfied. He claps his hands together and changes the subject. "My master has inconvenienced you terribly. I'll keep a very close eye on him, so he doesn't have a chance to make another appearance at the festival. Why don't we all call it a day here?"

"Huh? Um, but the final match... For the swordsmanship contest..."

"That's right, I'm the masked warrior Claw."

"What kind of pseudonym is that? It sounds like you got careless and started to write your real name, then twisted it into an alias at the last minute. I am very close to punching you, Master Claude. Forfeit the match. You've already had more than enough fun."

"Huh? But I wanted to fight the demon king..."

When Claude hears Auguste, he turns around, even though Keith has already grabbed him by the scruff of the neck. Restraining Keith for a moment, he faces Auguste. "You win."

"Huh?"

"When I fought with my left hand, I lost to you. That means you're the champion."

Although Beelzebuth was about to follow Claude, he turns around, looking irked. "But he's only a human. Is he strong?"

"He has talent. In terms of swordplay alone, he's even with you, Bel."

"He's what?! Hey, you! Someday, we're going to settle this!"

"Huh? Um, okay! Actually, who are you?!"

"Beelzebuth! Remember that name."

"Yes, yes, let's not cause them any more trouble. We're going home."

"Oh, before that." Claude snaps his fingers. The fallen church agents vanish, and the demolished stone lanterns disappear as well, down to the last fragment. The arena has been damaged in quite a few places, but particles of light envelop it, restoring everything to their original condition.

It's magic.

An impressed *Ooooooooh* rises from the spectators.

"That should do. Now then, shall we depart?" Claude rises lightly into the air, and Beelzebuth spreads his wings. Keith is also floating, but he doesn't look surprised. He's probably used to flying with Claude's magic.

"I'll leave the rest to you. Take care of it, and I'll forgive you for the matter of insulting Aileen— Learning your identity will have to come another time." He says that last comment while looking straight at Aileen. Her expression stiffens. Then Claude flies away, taking Keith and Beelzebuth with him.

"Is it over...?"

"Looks like."

"Um... So I'm the champion?"

Although the audience had been delighted by the magic, now that one of the finalists has made himself scarce, they've started murmuring in confusion. Just as she's wondering how to best deal with this, she hears a voice from a new direction.

"I heard an incredible racket, so I came to look into it, and what do I find...?"

"James!"

"How did the final match turn out?"

Stammering, Auguste somehow manages to explain. Walt cleverly glosses over the "show" by saying it was something they'd planned on their own.

"The guard unit challenged the demon king? Where's the sense in that?"

"I know, you're absolutely right. I'm sorry about all this. How should we wrap this up, President? The demon king took everyone who was running the contest away with him."

"...In that case, why don't we simply change the format? Make it a battle royale, say."

"Huh? Wait, but I won my way up here...!"

"We can settle the whole thing that way. It's fine, Auguste. You can still win this."

"Ehhhh?!" Auguste cries out in protest.

However, James mercilessly displays the full extent of his abilities, and the final becomes a chaotic melee, in which everyone who previously lost comes back, and they all go after Auguste.

"Arrrrgh! This was a disaster from day one!"

Uncharacteristically, Auguste complains, and the rest smile wryly. The first day of the school festival is over, and the members of the student council are in the guard room, savoring the hot herbal tea Rachel's prepared.

"You won. All's well that ends well, isn't it?"

"That's right. Better yet, you're practically unscathed."

"It got incredibly messy and ugly, though. Everyone chased me around, and it was scary."

"Oh, that's fine. You wouldn't think it, but that's what actual battlefields are like." Maybe because he's relaxed, Walt's gotten a bit careless about what he lets slip, but Aileen doesn't point it out to him. They've managed to avoid the event flag that triggers James's transformation. She doesn't want to be tactless in their moment of victory.

"By the way, where's Serena?"

"It looks like she went home. As far as she's concerned, tomorrow's the big day."

"Oh... That's when Princess Lily White gets chosen... The ball... Tomorrow's going to be busy, too..."

"Stop whining. Shape up."

The ever-optimistic Auguste is grousing, and James, who always put a damper on things, is trying to motivate him in his own way. Aileen feels like she's just caught a glimpse of an unexpected side to both of them and smiles to herself... *That's right. I mustn't assume I know them just because I know the game.* Even Walt and Kyle had accepted her reckless request and fought the demon king alongside her. That would've been impossible in the game. The characters she knew would definitely have carried out the church's orders, although they might have felt sad or tried to resist as they did it.

"Well, at any rate, we'll just have to give it our best again tomorrow. We still don't know where the demon snuff is coming from, and the matter of Ashtart hasn't been resolved either."

"True."

"I'd really prefer to call off the dressing-as-ducks part of this plan, though," Kyle grumbles.

Auguste laughs. "Come to think of it, people have been talking about how amazing those three ducks performed during the swordsmanship contest. We'll have to try harder too, won't we, James?"

"While dressed as ducks? Don't even joke about that."

As she drinks her tea, Aileen watches them. They're bantering with great fanfare, like ordinary students. An idea she's had for a while now suddenly comes into sharp focus. *I want all of them. I should introduce them to Jasper soon... I'll explain as much of the situation as I can to Rachel as well.*

Events are definitely no longer following the original game script. Once she's dealt with the matters of Ashtart and the demon snuff, she wants to give everything she's seen and learned some serious thought.

However, just before the closing event, an incident occurs.

"The prize for winning the title of Princess Lily White is pure demon snuff?!"

"Well, it is according to the anonymous letter that just turned up at my newspaper, at least."

It's past noon on the second day of the school festival, and Jasper has come to the guard room to deliver a report. He's out of breath. Luc and Quartz are already present. So is Isaac, of course, as well as the student council members, who've removed the heads of their duck costumes for the moment. Rachel is helping by serving tea.

"First the swordsmanship contest and now the ball...? Demon snuff really gets around, doesn't it?"

"If it's an anonymous letter, then you most likely don't have any idea where it's from."

"Right. It's just...if it's a false report, it's pretty spooky that it came to my paper, isn't it? Ailee—"

"Ailey," Luc whispers to Jasper.

Jasper adjusts his beret on his head, nodding. "Ailey, right. Anyway, it's like they're practically begging us to tell you. And considering the content, well... What do you want to do?" Jasper hands her the letter.

Behind him, Auguste whispers to James, "Ailey is friends with adults, too. Wow. So this is what secret organizations are like."

"It must be nice to be so simpleminded."

"That's the journalist Ailey's on good terms with, hmm? What do you think, Kyle?"

"...The real question is, who in the world is Ailey? Seriously."

"Say, your group's suddenly gotten a whole lot bigger. Who are these guys?" Jasper, who notices the whispering, aims his question at Isaac.

"New lackey candidates," Isaac tells him tersely.

"When they've still got their whole lives ahead of 'em... I guess we should give it our best shot. If anything comes up, feel free to talk it over with your uncle Jasper."

Jasper thumps James and the others on the shoulders. The expressions they're wearing defy description.

The prize for Princess Lily White Lily is uncut demon snuff.

That's all the letter says. After reading it through again, Aileen turns to Walt. "Do you know anything about this? Demon snuff in its purest form is dangerous, and it's not easy to get."

"If you're asking about the church leadership, after yesterday's fiasco, they're in no shape to pull anything like this. Kyle, have you heard anything?"

"No, nothing. We should confiscate the prize and inspect it soon as we can, though."

"Not possible." James cuts the suggestion down. "It's already at the contest venue, but there's a rule that the prize absolutely can't be opened until this year's Princess Lily White is chosen. Even if we tried to investigate it quietly, there is a security detail. A student tried to steal the prize once, so it's become routine to keep it under a tight watch."

"It would be tough to explain matters so convincingly that

we could inspect it openly... Would a demand from the student council do the trick?"

"Probably not. The swordsmanship contest is under the jurisdiction of the church, but the selection of Princess Lily White falls to the Ladies of the White Lily. Those judges are extremely particular. If the contents turn out to be dangerous, they're sure to cause a scene."

Auguste folds his arms, thinking hard. "What about getting Princess Lily White to show it to us? Then we'll have her hand it over."

"The top candidate for Princess Lily White is Serena Gilbert, isn't it? We can try asking her, I suppose...," Kyle says, but Aileen shakes her head.

"That leaves too much to chance, and we'd lose the initiative as well. Isn't there anything we can do now?"

"Um... May I...?" Rachel timidly raises her hand. Back when everyone had assembled, they'd explained to Rachel that a dangerous drug known as demon snuff was in circulation among the male student body and they were investigating it. "I may not understand this completely, but... You want Princess Lily White's prize, don't you, Master Ailey?"

"Yes, that's right."

"Then... Shall I enter the contest? I—I don't know whether I'll manage to win, but..."

Aileen claps her hands together in sudden realization. "That's it! That's exactly it, Rachel. Can I ask you to do that?!"

"Y-yes. If it will help, I'll give it my best!"

"Is that even going to work? You're sure you won't just collapse the second you get up onstage? Your social skills don't seem that solid." Isaac's eyebrows are drawn together in an approximation of a frown.

Rachel argues back boldly. "I—I can do it! I may not look it, but I am the daughter of a count!"

"We do have somebody else who's qualified, but... In any case, I guess there's not much choice but to go with this."

"What do you mean by 'not much choice'?! A-and besides, who else is qualifi—?"

"People were already saying Rachel is Serena's main rival in the contest. I think it'll be fine!" Auguste looks to the rest of the group for agreement, and Walt nods.

"It could work."

"No objections from me."

"I don't care what you do. If it comes down to it, we'll just negotiate with whoever becomes Princess Lily White."

With the academy's current tenants talking this way, even Isaac can't argue. He exhales heavily, shoulders slumping. "Then I guess it'll have to do. Just for the record, what's your take on this, Luc?"

"I'm not a student, so I'll leave the decision to those who are."

"...Practically speaking, it's the only option."

"Your uncle Jasper's in favor of this plan, too. Oh, but what about your outfit? Are you covered in that department, young lady?"

Rachel looks flustered. "You're right. My dress and cosmetics are... Oh no, I sold my dress..."

"It's all right. We'll make it in time for the ball this evening. Jasper, I imagine you can find us a good dress through your connections. Rachel, you go pick out your accessories with Isaac."

"Huh? W-with Isaac...?!"

"Why me? That sounds like a right pain."

"You're very trend-conscious. This is your field; I won't let you say you can't do it."

Seeing how flustered Rachel looks, Isaac clicks his tongue in irritation. "Fine, fine. Let's get going, old man."

"Just you leave it to me. All right, young lady, shall we depart?"

"O-of course. But...are you sure this is all right? I mean...the dress..."

"It's fine. Oh, as for the cosmetics, will Oberon Trading Firm products do?"

"Huh? ...Y-you have some?! I'd heard you couldn't get them outside the capital!"

Rachel's eyes are shining. Aileen wants to help her, and she nods cheerfully. Behind her, Luc and Quartz get up to go fetch the beauty products.

Attendance at the ball isn't mandatory, but contestants for Princess Lily White must register on the day of the festivities. At registration, they're simply given a number. The contestant isn't required to apply in person, so Aileen goes to complete the procedures. Then she waits for Rachel, holding a round card with #7 written on it.

We registered at the last minute, so it should be safe to assume there will be seven candidates. Who'd have thought there would be demon snuff in the prize for Princess Lily White, instead of the swordsmanship contest... Uncut stuff, at that.

The effects of demon snuff change depending on its concentration. In its purest form, it's practically a poisonous gas. Exposure to it would cause both humans and demons to lose their reason and lash out indiscriminately. If James gets even a whiff, he's bound to become a demon.

Nothing even resembling this had happened in the game. Not only that, but after yesterday's incident, the church should have washed its hands of the matter. In other words, there's a strong possibility that the source of this demon snuff is Ashtart. If all goes well, Aileen and the others would manage to resolve several issues with a single stroke. Even more incentive to retrieve it.

"Master Ailey! I'm sorry for the delay!"

They weren't able to secure a dressing room, so Rachel has been changing in the guard room. She finally steps out into the corridor.

Her dress is lovely, like pale pink petals unfurling. The design is generously draped, and it accentuates Rachel's gentle features brilliantly. There are diamonds decoratively sown into the seams of the dress here and there, and their faint sparkle almost resembles the fluttering wings of brand-new butterflies.

W-wow, Isaac's impressive as always…! The very latest fashion, just the way it was in the game art! Actually, is this going to be all right?! If I recall, the villainess is condemned during the Princess Lily White event…!

Out of a desire to be chosen as Princess Lily White, Rachel had made spiteful comments about Serena to the judges as well as various people around her and had ultimately tried to push her down the stairs. However, Serena had shrugged it all off, modified her torn dress, and marched onstage anyway. Her dignified bearing had won her acclaim from everyone present, while Rachel had been harshly criticized for her underhanded behavior.

Since Rachel only decided to participate on the day of the contest, she hasn't had time to do any of that. Most of all, Aileen knows quite well she isn't the type of person who would do those things to begin with, but she can't afford to be optimistic. In her dress, Rachel is identical to that game art, and it's impossible not to feel uneasy.

"Um... Does it not suit me?" Rachel tilts her head anxiously. Her hair has been put up in a loose chignon. Aileen shakes her head emphatically, hoping to dispel Rachel's concerns.

"N-no, it does. It suits you so well I couldn't stop staring."

"I thought it might be a little gaudy for me, but...Isaac said a bit of 'oomph' was ideal." Rachel looks bashful, but then she squeezes her hands into fists. "I'm going to give it my best! I know I don't look it, but I'm particularly good at etiquette... I—I do have social skills, you know. I'll leave Isaac absolutely speechless, you'll see!"

"...Rachel. Just out of curiosity..."

"Yes? What is it?"

"If you do become Princess Lily White, are you going to choose Isaac as your partner for the last dance?"

After a short pause, Rachel blushes so deeply her face practically catches fire. When she sees that, Aileen bursts out laughing. Rachel glares at her, red-faced. "That's not— Master Ailey, no! I—I intend to name you as my..."

"No, since you've got the opportunity, why not go with Isaac?"

"Oh, I couldn't! I-I'm sure he'd find it an absolute nuisance. He won't give me the time of day, really..."

"Can I ask what it is about him?" Aileen holds out her hand. It's quite a long way from here to the venue. With Rachel in that dress, she may very well trip without some help.

"...When I brought up breaking off my engagement, my

parents were very much against it, and of course my fiancé was incredibly angry with me. People blamed me for all sorts of things, and I wondered if I'd truly made the right choice. There was no longer any place for me, even at home."

Engagements between aristocrats were contracts between their respective families. It was no wonder they'd all thought Rachel was being selfish.

"However, when I reported the fact that I'd managed to dissolve the engagement, Isaac told me I'd done the right thing. That was all. Still, I felt terribly proud of myself."

Pressing her lips together, Rachel looks forward. In that moment, her face is just lovely.

"That's why I'll do everything I can this time as well. Whether I look it or not, I am perfectly capable of intrigue."

"Are you really?"

"Yes. Lady Serena's etiquette is a little careless. It does give her an incredible talent for attracting attention, but... To compensate, I intend to have Master James dance with me. That alone will be enough to make me stand out. Then, since the judges are strict and finicky about etiquette, everyone seems to be trying to avoid them, so I think I'll come from the opposite angle and actively appeal to them directly."

As Rachel works out her plan of attack, determined not to lose, Aileen sees something of her past self in the young girl. The social pariah who dared to attend that soiree. She pins the tag with the number to Rachel's bodice, placing it carefully so it won't detract from her beauty.

"Do your best. We're counting on you."

"I will!— Oh."

Speak of the devil: Serena is descending the stairs from the upper landing. She's still in her school uniform, carrying her dress. When she sees Rachel, her eyes widen. "Rachel. You're wearing a number. Does that mean you're entering the Princess Lily White competition? I'd heard you weren't..."

"Yes. I changed my mind." Rachel smiles. That confident expression makes her look very much like a villainess. Aileen takes a step back, watching the villainess and heroine confront each other. She has no part to play in this particular scene.

It keeps her from reacting in time.

"I see! Let's both give it our best. Oh, and that dress is splendid! Let me get a better look at— Eek!"

"Rachel!"

Serena has artlessly touched Rachel's dress, but then she pulls on it, and they both fall.

Aileen hears another student say, "Someone just fell down the stairs!"

Hastily, she runs over to them. They're lying on the landing.

"Rachel, are you all right?!"

"Master...Ailey. Y-yes. I'm fine...ngh!"

Rachel tries to move her leg, then winces. However, Serena speaks up first. "Ouch... Oh no, my dress!"

The lace on the dress Serena was holding is torn.

"Lady Serena fell?"

"It sounds like the other girl's fine. Serena's dress got ripped, though."

"The competition hasn't started yet. Do you suppose she was pushed?"

"That girl's a member of the guard. Lately she's been bragging about how she broke off her engagement..."

"Wait a—"

Half-formed guesses begin flying immediately. Aileen tries to speak up, but Rachel catches her arm and shakes her head. She knows that any protests they make will only end up fueling the commotion. If things are allowed to progress, though, it will end just like the game.

Besides, Aileen saw it.

"...R-Rachel. Please don't worry about it. This was all an accident. I can do something about my dress."

Just before they fell down the stairs, Serena had yanked on Rachel's skirts.

"Let's make this a good, fair contest!"

She'd seen her fall intentionally, with a twisted smile on her lips.

This woman—!

Serena gets up, pretending to wince over her scrapes and scratches, and looks down at them with a triumphant smile. Rachel can't stand on her own; Aileen is supporting her. Turning her back on them both, she jauntily leaves the landing.

"Hey, Ailey, what happened— Rachel?"

"I heard someone fell. Don't tell me..."

Just as Serena vanishes from sight, Isaac appears, accompanied by Walt in his duck costume. They've been patrolling the school halls right up until the last minute.

Rachel's face is pale, but she's trying to stand. "I-I'm all right. I can...do it—agh."

"Rachel, I'm pretty sure you've twisted that ankle."

"O-only a little bit. It should still support me. I'm all right."

"Uh, you're wobbling. You can't dance like that. Winning the title of Princess Lily White isn't gonna happen."

"No, but—! I-I-I'm all right. Even if it isn't much, I want to be useful to Master Ailey...!"

"Rachel. Would you lend me that dress?"

Rachel looks as if she's about to burst into tears, but Aileen's quiet proposal makes her blink. Walt's mouth falls open, and Isaac gazes up at the ceiling.

How dare you treat my sweet protégé like that?

It's time for a war by proxy. As a smile slowly dawns on Aileen's face, it makes her look every inch a villainess.

"There you are, James."

James has finally escaped from the duck costume and changed back into his uniform. He looks at Auguste, who's also shed his costume.

The flames in the silver candlesticks flicker like something out of a dream, and the chandeliers sparkle. Their light brightly illuminates Auguste's face. Behind them, an orchestra plays languidly. The closing ball has begun at last.

"What is it? I'm tired already."

"Ha-ha. Yes, we've had nothing but trouble since yesterday. Oh, Kyle! Good work today!"

"Thanks. Let's just pray that the Ashtart affair ends up being an empty prank, at least."

"I hear you there. Wait, where's Walt?"

"Here. We finally made it out of the ducks, didn't we? It doesn't look as though sweet Ailey's here yet, but..."

That topic makes James scowl. "Is he serious about dressing as a girl?"

"Ailey's really brave, isn't he?"

"To think he'd pull off everything from ducks to drag..."

"Mm... It might look surprisingly good on him, you know," Walt jokes.

"Are you insane?" James scoffs. "He may have a slim build, but he's still a man."

"Even if he manages to look like a girl, will he be all right as far as etiquette's concerned?"

"I hear extravagant dresses can be heavier than poorly made armor. Will he be able to move?"

"Well, I'm not expecting much myself. I do think it may be worth seeing, though."

"If he's unsightly, I'll throw him out personally. It'd be a disgrace to Misha Academy." James folds his arms, and everyone else smiles awkwardly. Then there's a stir in the crowd.

A girl in a gown as pure as a white lily steps gracefully through the main doors, under a shining chandelier. It's Serena.

An admiring sigh rises from the assembly. Walt whistles quietly. "No surprise; she looks gorgeous."

"She's entry number one, hmm? I take it she's thoroughly prepared. If there aren't any upsets, she'll probably wind up being named Princess Lily White... Should we negotiate for the prize with her in advance?" Kyle asks.

Auguste shakes his head. "Isaac says he doesn't want to leak any more information than we absolutely need to, right up until the end."

"...Meaning all we can do is watch."

"You're all here! It's rare to see the four of you together." Serena's noticed them, and she comes trotting over, beaming.

Now that she mentions it... They exchange looks. It didn't register as it was happening, but they've grown used to being a group.

"Things have been rather eventful lately."

"Heh-heh. Thanks to Ailey, we've all gotten rather close."

"That's all in your head. I'm not close to any of you," James denies gruffly.

"...Hmm?" When Serena tilts her head, her earrings sparkle. "Oh, right, of course—Auguste or President James, would you dance with me later? That should make me stand out."

"Oh, um... I have some guard duty, so..."

"...I also have a few things to do for the guard unit."

Remembering that he'll have more business to attend to once the ball begins in earnest, James looks weary. There are no girls he wants to dance with, so that part hardly matters, but a hassle is a hassle.

Oh, but Ailey said to dance with him first so he'd stand out... I'll be dancing with a man, then?

When Walt and Kyle turn her down as well, Serena plants her hands on her hips, puffing her cheeks out sulkily. "What's wrong with all of you? When did every last one of you become guards? I heard you were dressing like ducks, but that can't possibly be true, can it?"

"I exercise my right to remain silent."

"*Haaaah.* Ever since Ailey Calois joined, you've all been strange. Pull yourselves together."

They respond to Serena's lecture with vague smiles. They're probably feeling rather awkward.

I do think it's a hassle... But that's my business.

It would seem he isn't entirely averse to their current relationship after all. He'd really prefer to do without a friendship forged by duck costumes, but getting dragged around by Ailey has made something start to grow inside them... Even if each of them is still quite preoccupied with their own concerns and circumstances.

"If I invite you, you should oblige me! Gentlemen shouldn't embarrass a lady. All right, excuse me while I go pay my respects to the judges."

"Good luck, Serena— Oh, that's right. Is the demon king coming?"

Serena had been about to turn around, but stops the moment she hears Auguste's question. "It sounds as if he and his attendants are working outside the city today. I do hope he returns in time for the dance after Princess Lily White is chosen, but I don't know if he will..."

"After yesterday, that's probably to be expected. He's tightened security for us; there won't be any problems."

"I personally have a serious problem with it! Argh, honestly...! I'll see you later."

Turning her back on them, Serena marches off. It's good that she's energetic, but will she pass the etiquette inspection that way? The fact that she moves like that even in a formal gown is part of her charm, but still.

"Say... Won't there be trouble if Ailey doesn't turn up soon?" Auguste murmurs. He's looking at the wall clock that hangs in the great marble hall.

Kyle softly lowers his eyes. "Dressing as a woman may have been impossible after all."

"I'll go check on him." Feeling as if things are going nowhere, James steps away from the wall he's been leaning against. The others automatically begin to follow him.

"Why are the rest of you coming with me? We'll be conspicuous."

"We're all in the same boat, so why not? Besides, we're the Duck Squadron. Right, Blue?"

"Would you stop incessantly reminding me about the duc…"

Right as James trails off, Auguste walks right into his back. He starts to say "What gives?" but breaks off in the middle. Walt, who was smirking at them, stands there with his mouth hanging open, and Kyle freezes on the spot.

There is no noise or commotion. Only the quiet click of heels on the marble floor echoes through the room.

Pale pink skirts drift as lightly as a feather. A tag that reads #7 is fixed to a slender waist. It's the number Rachel Danis should have worn.

In other words, this is her proxy.

No way, someone murmurs. Is it Auguste, or possibly Walt?

Swallowing, his throat dry, James gazes at the figure.

"Good evening, everyone."

In the center of the silent venue, exuding the beauty of a glimmering star, she smiles.

When you walk, stay as light as an angel. No matter how heavy your gown may be, maintain your posture. Always wear an elegant smile. Pay attention to your bearing, from your toes to your fingertips. Steal everyone's eyes.

These lessons have been drummed into the very marrow of her bones. Even if she's spent quite a long time pretending to be a boy, Aileen can do them without even thinking.

Ensuring she has the attention of everyone in the hall is simple. While the academy is distinguished, this is just a provincial school festival, nothing more than students playing make-believe. She has competed ruthlessly in true high society, in the heart of the empire, and no one here is a match for her.

…Let alone someone who has to resort to methods as underhanded as pushing other candidates down the stairs.

"You are, erm…"

"Members of the review panel. I place myself in your ever-capable hands this evening."

Without so much as hinting at her identity, Aileen smiles and executes a flawless curtsy. It's so perfect it puts a textbook greeting to shame, and a sigh of admiration escapes the Ladies of the White Lily who are serving as judges.

"Gracious… Miss Number Seven, what lovely form."

"Thank you, Lady Royce. I studied using the book you authored, *The Rules and Radiance of Gentlewomen*. It was very easy to understand, and I've read it often."

"M-my. You've read my book? How marvelous."

"Lady Zeal, it's a pleasure to make your acquaintance. I heard you wore a similar gown to a recent soiree, and I ventured to model mine after it. It doesn't look strange, does it?"

"No, no, it suits you very well. You've made some improvisations around the waist, have you not?"

"Oh, you noticed! I'm so glad. Professor Gotham, it's an honor to meet you as well. I found your treatise on women's rights very intriguing. I would love to hear your views regarding a certain matter."

"Really now! And you're so young. That's quite admirable. What is it you'd like to know?"

"You see, I have always felt that the right to participate in politics is essential to improving the social standing of women…"

She smiles, politely greeting and conversing with each judge. It goes over so well that she guesses many students are incapable of doing even this much.

Even Lady Lilia managed to compete on this level, you know. Her manners and knowledge are lacking, but she's incredibly skilled at giving compliments and listening to people.

Serena may be a heroine as well, but she's no match for Aileen.

When she's finished greeting the panel of judges, who let her go only with great reluctance, Aileen casts a slow glance at Serena.

Serena's watching her, and her face is beet red. Her clenched fists are trembling.

By rights, she should have been competing with Rachel. Serena's etiquette is poor, but she has an abundance of charisma; Rachel has no trouble with etiquette, but she's a bit drab. It would probably have been a close contest. If she'd fought fairly, no matter what the results were, Aileen wouldn't have interfered.

However, this woman threw the match. In which case, if an outsider steps in and flattens her, she honestly can't complain.

On principle, when someone picks a fight with Aileen, she never turns it down.

As things stand, it's probably fortunate that portrait made the rounds. Even if they see what I really look like, no one's going to recognize me as Aileen Lauren d'Autriche.

Of course she's still planning to find and dispose of whoever distributed that portrait.

"You..."

A dazed voice calls to her, and she turns.

James, Auguste, Walt, Kyle. The members of the student council look like a bunch of wide-eyed pigeons who've all just been blasted by a peashooter.

"My, if it isn't the student council. Good evening. It's a lovely night, isn't it?"

"......"

"Is something the matter?"

When she smiles at them warmly, for some reason, the four of them turn their backs and start whispering to each other.

"Am I dreaming, Auguste? Pinch me— Ow... Seriously?"

"What do I do? It's not a dream... Whoa, wait, my heart's racing."

"I'd try to stop it, Auguste. That's a man, righ— Wait, is this a dream?"

"Heh-heh. Wow, this isn't like me at all. What should I do? It's way beyond anything I was expecting..."

Aileen can hear all of this, but she just watches them, smiling quietly.

"Um, what was it again? Weren't we supposed to do something?"

"Dance. We were supposed to ask her..."

"That's a man. I need to wake up!"

"No, Kyle, just calm down a minute. I'll try to calm down, too."

"...Was there something you needed to ask me?"

At this rate, they aren't going to get anywhere, so Aileen brings it up herself. Hearing her prompt, they all straighten up and freeze. *They are still students, I suppose. They can't even invite a girl to dance properly. Master Claude would have been a perfect escort, and yet...* However, if he bursts in here the way he had during the swordsmanship contest, she'll abandon everything—including her dignity—and flee.

"Um! Would y— Me! Would you dance with me?!" Auguste's hand shoots up.

Walt yelps. "Hey! Who said you could go first!"

"Something's...wrong with my eyes... I need to replace them—"

"Kyle, seriously, calm down! You're more bothersome than I remember!"

"Quit yelling, all of you. You're annoying... I'll dance."

"Ah—James, I asked first!"

"Shut up. There are several things I need to be sure of before I can relax again, that's all!"

Shaking off Auguste, who's wailing that it's not fair, James bows deferentially. "My lovely lady. Would you do me the honor of this dance?"

He isn't quite at Claude's level, but she'd expect no less from the final boss of the sequel. He's earned a passing grade. Aileen smiles and nods.

Rachel gazes at the figure from where she's standing by the wall of the great hall. The dress is so perfect, and the dance steps so lovely, that even though she's a bona fide lady, she feels rather defeated.

"He's even flawless at dressing as a woman... Master Ailey really is incredible."

He's dealing with James, Auguste, and the school's other popular male students, but he's still holding his own. Or rather, he's using them as stepping-stones to further his progress. As a matter of fact, the members of the student council are attracting envious looks. The majority of those eyes seem to belong to people who want to dance, not with James and the others, but with *her*.

Thanks to that, Rachel isn't getting as much attention as she'd feared.

"—Did you hear? They say Lady Serena was pushed down the stairs…"

"That's the girl who did it, right?"

The rumors have spread rapidly, but they don't burn her ears as much as she'd expected them to. Just as that thought occurs to her, a boy leans back against the wall beside her with a thump.

"Isaac…"

"Want a drink?" Isaac holds out a glass of punch. She thanks him, accepting it meekly.

"What are you doing here? You're hurt. You could just bail."

His brusque tone irks her. "Leaving would just be frustrating. I haven't done anything wrong after all."

"…Hm."

"I don't want to let her beat me that thoroughly." She doesn't specify who she means, but Isaac seems to get it. He nods, agreeing with her.

Why did I think somebody like that was dashing?

Rachel knows it's because that person isn't afraid to speak her mind, and she attracts attention. She's disgusted with herself for having idolized someone for such a flimsy reason.

Being truly attractive isn't anything so superficial.

"…Master Ailey is dashing, isn't he?" He never said he was doing it for Rachel. However, simply seeing him there is giving her courage. That's what she wants to be like.

"Dashing or not, he's definitely going to be named Princess Lily White. That's a huge help," Isaac says.

"He's a man, but he's prettier than I am."

"Uh… I don't think that's anything you need to worry about. Or, wait…maybe it is?"

"That sort of woman is my ideal, though. I won't get discouraged. I'll simply learn from him instead."

Isaac scratches his cheek, looking a little embarrassed. "...Don't overdo it. Okay, time for me to get back to my guard duty. I've got three partners left."

"Oh, that's right. You were dancing with five in all, weren't you?" As she says it, she lowers her eyes. In the end, she hadn't managed to become the sixth one.

I've sprained my leg, too. Maybe I should have at least asked him. If she had, even if they hadn't danced, perhaps the regret she felt wouldn't be so piercing. "Do your best, please. Master Ailey is counting on you."

"Nobody counts on me that much."

She blinks at him. Isaac gives an awkward smile. "Way back when, there was this girl whose dance partner stood her up. She was being a wallflower, all by herself, and I couldn't ask her to dance. Just like you, people were saying all sorts of stuff about her, but she refused to cry, and she acted like it didn't faze her. But that only made it harder for me to man up, somehow. What a coward, right?"

"...Huh? Um, wait, who are you talking about?"

"Me. I'm all brain, and I can't make a move when it actually matters."

"Th—that's not true!" Belatedly, Rachel realizes she's shouting. Isaac turns to look at her, startled. "Isaac, you've done all sorts of things for me and your friends! When someone needs help, you're always there for them. That's a terribly difficult thing to manage!"

Even now, he's standing beside Rachel to shield her from the rumors and the questioning looks. There's no way anyone like that could be a coward. It makes her oddly angry, and she glares at him. "That girl didn't need to be helped at that exact moment, that's all. You were simply able to see that. Isaac, you're—"

Although he may have wanted to help her anyway.

The moment that thought occurs to her, her heart feels as heavy as if she's swallowed lead. She nearly looks down. But then she raises her head, thinking, *So what?* It's just then she realizes that's probably what it means to be gallant.

"You are incredibly dashing! Hold your head high!"

"O-okay…" Isaac nods, as if she's overawed him. Rachel breathes in, then out, so deeply that her shoulders rise and fall. He blinks at her several times, but then he cracks up quietly. "Look, if you're gonna do this, become a different kind of beauty. Don't be like that one."

"What…?"

"Anyway, thanks. I feel better." With one last gentle smile, he leaves. Belatedly, shame sweeps over Rachel. *Wh-what am I even saying…! How embarrassing!*

"Why, if it isn't Rachel! Wearing your school uniform to a ball? What's the matter?"

That voice clears Rachel's mind instantly. "…Lady Serena."

"Oh! Wait, was your dress ruined? You can hide minor damage with a few modifications, though. See?" Serena flutters her white dress, flaring it out.

Conscious of the glances people are stealing at them, Rachel gives her a polite smile. "I—I think it looks quite splendid… Um, did you need something?"

"Well, I mean, I was worried about the wallflower in her school uniform." Serena peeks at her face. Rachel can see her own expression reflected in her eyes.

Worried? No, that's not it. She wants to see how frustrated I am.

If she does, she can bask in the feeling that she's won. Rachel clenches her fists. She puts on a smile. "I'm fine. I have my guard duty anyway."

"...Hm. Really? Well, that might not be bad either. I think I'll excuse myself soon."

"What? But they haven't selected Princess Lily White yet."

"Oh, Princess Lily White is sure to be that girl. Although I couldn't tell you who she is." She jerks her chin in the direction of the mysterious young noblewoman in the pale pink gown.

"I wonder if she had an in with someone. Does she go to this school? Do you know her?"

"N-no."

"Now that I think about it, though, I'm not really the Princess Lily White type. Besides, it does look as if Master Claude won't be able to make it. In that case, the title should go to whoever wants it."

"......"

"At any rate, I have a more important duty to carry out. Oh, have you seen Auguste?"

"He mentioned wanting to get some fresh air. I think he went outside a minute ago," she tells her, feeling perplexed.

"I see," Serena responds. "All right, Rachel. Do enjoy the ball." She smiles at the other girl, with her school uniform and her sprained ankle, unable to be anything more than a wallflower. That smile oozes superiority. Rachel draws a breath.

"—It is embarrassing to have them announce that you can't be Princess Lily White in front of everyone, isn't it?"

Serena's smile vanishes. Looking her straight in the eye,

Rachel smiles. "I know how you feel. If I were in your position, Lady Serena, I might run away myself."

The possibility that she'd strike back must never have occurred to Serena. Someone she thought was roundly inferior has just snapped at her, and her angry gaze stabs into Rachel, but Rachel meets it boldly.

She won't let her quit while she's ahead.

At last, Serena gives a brief response, practically spitting it out. "...I'm pleased you understand."

She stalks off. Relieved, Rachel exhales.

She doesn't know whether she's won or lost. However, she's managed not to suffer a total defeat.

...That's right. I did my best. Next time, I'll be able to ask Isaac to dance. I'm sure I will.

She'll work up the courage. She'll be as dashing as the person who's standing on the platform now.

"—We will now announce this year's Princess Lily White. Entry number seven!"

After all, he must be putting in a lot of work in order to make winning look so easy.

Aileen had been confident, but the moment she hears the announcement, she's relieved. Accepting Princess Lily White's crown and bouquet, she acknowledges the applause with a curtsy.

The fact that Serena isn't on the platform concerns her, but the prize comes first.

"This is the gift that the lucky lady named Princess Lily White will receive this year."

The prize has been brought in on a cart. Snatching it up, Aileen backs away. "Next, Princess Lily White will select her partner for the last—"

"All right, if you'll excuse me!"

"Huh? P-Princess Lily White?!"

Leaping lightly down from the stage, she sprints straight across the ballroom. Startled by her sudden move, the crowd parts.

She can't afford to stay on that stage and field all sorts of prying questions about her identity. As they'd agreed, Rachel is waiting for her just outside the hall, which is rapidly growing noisier.

"Master Ailey, this way, over here! Change in this room."

"Thanks, Rachel."

Rachel has been shielding the door from view. Sliding through it, Aileen promptly strips off her gown. Although it's no way to treat an expensive dress, she stuffs it into the bag that has her change of clothes in it. She removes her makeup, binds her chest, puts her hair in a bun, hides it under her wig, and pulls on her boys' uniform.

"You there! You're, uh...one of the guards? Have you seen Princess Lily White?"

"N-no, I haven't!"

"What are we going to do about the last dance? Running off like that— The Ladies of the White Lily are furious."

"Hey, over here! Hurry up!"

That voice belongs to Isaac, and he leads the other students off.

Once the patter of footsteps has receded, Aileen cautiously peeks out of the room.

Rachel looks relieved, but then her expression grows oddly conflicted.

"What? Does something still look strange?"

"No... You're Master Ailey, the same as always, but... Now that I'm paying attention, your features are rather feminine, aren't they?"

"Huh?!"

"Ailey...?"

Walt has stepped out of the great hall, and at the sound of his voice, she turns around. Kyle and James are there as well. Gratefully, she breaks off her conversation with Rachel. "How is it in there, you two?"

"How else? There's a huge uproar..." Partway through James's answer, there's a peculiar shift in his expression, and he averts his eyes.

"What's the matter?"

"Nothing. It's just sort of, you know..."

"...Walt. Am I awake? What are these palpitations? He's a man..."

"Kyle, come on, calm down. The prize is what matters now."

The others have been fidgeting, but at Walt's remark, they clear their throats or turn to face her again, repeating "He's a man, he's a man," like a mantra. Aileen is perplexed, but she opens the box she's been holding.

"When pure demon snuff is exposed to air, it turns into a gas," Walt warns her. "It's probably been encased in wax for storage purposes. Be careful not to break that."

Nodding, she opens the inner case. Inside, she finds a small ceramic censer.

Kyle murmurs. "It's of eastern make. That's an incense burner."

"So the demon snuff is inside it?"

"Inside, there's...nothing. It's empty."

The tension in the air vanishes instantly. With the lid of the censer unclasped, Aileen thinks hard. She turns it upside down, but nothing comes out. All she knows is that it's a fine piece of work, with delicate ornamentation and a painting of a dragon.

"...Then that letter really was just a prank?" Walt is gazing at the censer.

James looks dubious. "One that was delivered to Ailey's journalist acquaintance by sheer coincidence? It's too convenient."

"That journalist is usually in the capital, isn't he? Don't tell me—has something happened there?"

"If it had, I think we would have gotten word..."

Everything they're coming up with is nothing more than conjecture, but Aileen has a bad feeling about this.

It's as if we're being toyed with. Not only that, but the capital... Could the source of the demon snuff be there, too?

If so, she'll have to reexamine this situation from the very beginning.

"By the way, where's Auguste?" She's just realized she hasn't seen him. Everyone looks at each other.

"He said he was tired from dancing and was stepping out for some air, and he never came back."

"Oh, I saw Lady Serena go out after Master Auguste. She said she had business with him."

"Serena did?"

"They may be together," Rachel tells her.

James looks thoughtful. "Come to think of it, she slipped out of the Princess Lily White review as well. Should we look for her?"

"If Serena's confessing her love to Auguste, we'll make things very awkward." Walt's concern is valid, but she has a strange sense of foreboding about all this.

As Ailey hesitates, unable to make up her mind, Rachel catches her sleeve. "Master Ailey, look. Isn't that them?"

Everyone looks in the direction Rachel's pointing. Serena, still in her gown, is pulling Auguste into the great hall. The room is still crowded with students.

"They appear to be back."

"Let's go. Serena was holding something. Rachel, you go call Isaac."

"A-all right."

When Aileen starts down the hall, the rest follow her.

It looked like a small perfume bottle, but... No, it couldn't be...

Growing impatient, she breaks into a jog. Just as she passes through the large double doors—the same ones she ran out of a few minutes earlier—Serena's voice rings out. "Tonight, I have an announcement to make."

Noticing Aileen and the others, Auguste turns around. He looks bewildered. Beside him, Serena speaks slowly. "Ashtart is here, in this academy, and I am about to unmask him."

That wild remark sets the room buzzing. However, Serena seems unconcerned. Taking a slow look around the assembly, she throws her shoulders back and continues in a clear, ringing voice.

"A demon is lurking among your fellow students. That's a very dreadful thing, but I will be brave and accuse him."

"Serena, listen... You're acting kind of funny. You called me a Holy Knight or something..."

When she hears Auguste's remark, Aileen's eyes widen in

shock. *A Holy Knight?! How does Serena know— It can't be! Is she like me?!*

"I have been charged with the mission of exposing and passing judgment upon him…" Serena raises her arm high. When they see what she has in her hand, both Walt and Kyle make a dive for it.

"Uncut demon snuff—"

"…as the agent of the Maid of the Sacred Sword."

Wearing a blissful smile, Serena lets the perfume bottle fall.

The glass shatters, and malevolent-looking smoke billows up from the marble floor.

As the sweet, suffocating smell spreads, Walt shouts, "Poison! Everyone out of the hall!"

Screams go up. The students all make a rush for the door, and sheer chaos erupts in the hall. The important thing is to get away as quickly as possible. If they only breathe in a little, it won't be addictive, and any effects will be mild and temporary. Kyle yells, too, spurring them on. "Get out fast, and don't breathe in any of that stuff! You'll die!"

"President James…! Pull yourself together!" Buffeted by the crowd, James staggers, and Aileen hastily supports him. As soon as she touches him, she feels the demon-slaying sacred sword react inside her. *I have to purify him… I can't keep up!* Thick demon snuff smoke is streaming toward them, almost as if it's targeting James. His eyes are unfocused, and his body keeps emitting odd cracking noises. Horns and wings sprout, as if they're eating their way out from inside him. *It's no use, I can't stop it— He's going to turn into a demon!*

"So it was you, President James?"

The students have fled, and a delighted voice echoes in the now-empty ballroom.

Aileen bites her lip. Next to Serena, Auguste speaks up, his voice trembling. "James… You… Those things…"

James flinches. It's as if he's frightened.

At the same time, Aileen hears the sound of guns being leveled. It's Walt and Kyle, behind them. Immediately she spreads her arms, shielding James. "Walt. Kyle. Stop this."

"We kill demons—"

"—Even if they used to be our friends."

"So Kyle and Walt really are the church's hunters, sent to slay the demon!" Serena sounds impressed. Her comment pulls Walt's and Kyle's attention toward her. They shut their mouths, as if they're swallowing something bitter.

All by herself, Serena speaks euphorically, like a true believer who's finally received a divine revelation. "Now then, Auguste, hurry! You will become a Holy Knight. I'll help you. Kill the demon, for all of us! Even Master Claude will be glad if Ashtart is dealt with."

"The church? ...Ah. So you came to kill me?" James straightens up unsteadily. "I see. Then..." There's self-mockery in James's eyes, something very close to absolute despair. For just a moment, Aileen sees it. "Then you—all of you—were tricking me this whole time?"

"No—"

A roar that sounds like laughter whips up a blast of wind, blowing the hall to pieces. It sends Aileen flying as well; she crashes into the remnants of a wall that's been reduced to rubble and gets the wind knocked out of her.

In the meantime, gunshots ring out. She hears screams from the students who've fled outside. James, Walt, and Kyle have started to fight.

"Wait— Just a secon...!"

"Ailey, are you okay?" Auguste runs over to her and helps her up.

In the distance, Serena is screaming, "What is your problem?! I can't believe this! Auguste, bring out the sacred sword and kill him! Hurry up!"

"Look— There's something wrong with you! What are you talking about? What sacred sword?!"

"It's fine, Auguste, you can do it! I know you can!" Serena smiles; she looks absolutely positive. Even if that's her game knowledge talking, something's off.

Lilia only lends Auguste the sacred sword. It's not something he has...

But James comes first. That blast dispersed the demon snuff in the air, and he still recognizes Aileen and the others. There's a chance she'll be able to purify him—but James is blinded by anger. She has to stop him!

"President James! Please don't do this!"

James's red eyes turn to her. Then he rushes straight at her. There's no emotion in those eyes. When she sees his long, sharp claws bearing down on both of them, Aileen shoves Auguste out of the way.

"Ailey!"

"James, you—!"

"Walt, no, don't shoot, you'll hit Ailey!"

Heat slashes across her chest in a slanting line. Her uniform jacket and the fabric she's wrapped around herself split open. When James sees that, his expression returns. "A...girl...?!"

He stops moving for a moment, and she grabs his wrist and screams at him, "James, come back!"

That hand is the one she'd hold the sacred sword with, and light explodes from it. James howls like a cornered animal. At the center of the blast, although the wind tears at her clothes, Aileen stands her ground. She hadn't secured her wig properly; it flies off, and her shining blond hair streams out behind her.

"Let go, let go, let go, let me gooooo!!" James shrieks and struggles. She can feel a rejection of the purification through the hand she's holding. Emotions flood into her.

Being hunted, living wretchedly, nights when his fear of death wouldn't let him sleep. He'd curled up, hugging his knees, refusing to die like this. Why did he have to be killed? There had to be a place for him somewhere, anywhere. *Live proudly.* His parents had died so he could have a chance to live.

But he knows. He's neither demon nor human, and he's sure there's no place for him anywhere.

Sacred sword, don't! You mustn't kill him!

The sacred sword exists to slay demons, and it's trying to manifest against Aileen's will. She can't let it happen. If the demon king so much as touched the sacred sword for a moment, even he would be blown away. If James does it, there won't be anything left of him.

"Let me go! Why?! Why do I have to be killed?!"

"I told you I would protect you, didn't I?! Believe in me!"

James's eyes widen.

"I refuse to let you turn into a demon and get yourself killed! If you have no place to belong, that's fine! Just stay with me!"

She is the woman who will marry the demon king. She can't afford to lose to a thing like the sacred sword, no matter what!

"Believe in me and let me in, James!!"

The blinding light is drawn into James's body. The black wings on his back turn into particles of light and scatter.

She exhales sharply, releasing him.

"…Ailey!"

Aileen has toppled backward, and Auguste catches her without hesitating. Through half-open eyes, Aileen makes out James's form on the ground. There are no horns on his head anymore, and his wings have vanished. He seems to be back to normal.

Thank goodness. I never dreamed he'd be more trouble than Master Claude's dragon form…

It's probably a matter of physical difference. Claude is completely human, but James's body is half demon. No doubt the transformation is easier for him. She should have expected no less from the final boss of Game 2.

"I'm all right. Help James…"

"My dear Ailey… What in the world are y—?"

"What…was *that*? What just happened?!"

There's a shrill shriek, and everyone looks at Serena.

"Auguste, what about the sacred sword?! Besides, look, he's still alive—" At the sound of a gun being cocked directly behind her head, her energetic voice trails off.

Kyle has circled around behind Serena and is holding her at gunpoint. "Answer my question first. Why did you have demon snuff?" he mutters.

"De…demon snuff? What's that?"

"Play dumb if you like. The church's idea of torture is no joke, Serena."

"Wh-what's that supposed to mean? I don't even— I don't know— He's the demon, remember?! All of this is his fault!" Serena points at James. He's gotten to his feet, his face pale.

Auguste is the first to respond. "You know that's not true. This is all your doing, Serena!"

"A-Auguste...?"

"James hasn't done a single thing wrong! You're the one who turned him into a demon!"

James's vacant face turns toward Auguste.

Serena's expression stiffens. "He's always been a demon... Walt! Say something to them! You'd never ally yourself with a demon, would you?!"

"Of course not. But we aren't your allies, either."

"...Besides, right now, James is human. No one's ordered us to kill humans."

They're clearly splitting hairs. However, it's pretty clear they don't want to kill James.

James must have picked up on this. He blinks, just once.

"You're joking, that's... That can't be right, can it?! I—I only—"

"Hey, what's that?!" someone shouts, drowning out Serena's rambling. The hall James demolished hardly counts as an indoor space anymore.

"I guess we'll talk later. All right, Serena. For now, you're coming with us."

"Wait, Walt. Look at that—up there." Kyle points at the darkening sky. Aileen looks where he's pointing, and her eyes widen.

A stunned silence falls, but only for a moment. Almost immediately, the students start screaming.

"Demons!"

"Why are demons...? Wait, is that Ashtart?!"

"—Oh, hell! Serena!"

While Walt is distracted, Serena makes a break for it. She vanishes into the chaos erupting around them, and Walt can't run after her. He clicks his tongue in frustration.

"Damn it!"

"Dealing with the demons comes first, Walt. They're being drawn here by the demon snuff, and this won't be the last of them."

"Well, sure, if she's going to splash uncut stuff around with wild abandon!"

The shifting swarm of demons practically blots out the sky. They're headed straight for them. That horrible smoke was blown away by James's attack, but its distinctive aroma still hangs thick in the air.

The demons' eyes are glittering in an abnormal way. They've probably lost their sanity.

This couldn't be worse. Aileen exhales, then breathes in. She gets to her feet. "...All of you, run. I'll do something about them."

"What are you saying, Ailey?"

"Almond. The rest of you, too. No matter what happens to me, you mustn't come out." The scent of demon snuff drives demons insane. Right now, this place is unspeakably dangerous for them.

Kyle frowns at Aileen, who's speaking to her shadow in the moonlight. "What are you talking about? Never mind that, hurry up and run."

"Unfortunately, I'm not so weak that I need you to protect me. Go help the students evacuate the area first."

She sweeps her hair back, drawing herself up to her full height. "Oh, of course." She smiles at them. "I hadn't introduced myself yet. I am Aileen Lauren d'Autriche."

She focuses her power in her right hand. As the light changes into a dazzling sword, everyone stares.

However, demons who've lost their minds probably won't recoil from it.

Sacred sword, you mustn't kill, she tells it silently.

"I am the woman who will be the demon king's wife."

She won't kill demons. She'll protect humans as well.

That's the sort of person the Maid of the Cursed Sword wants to be.

In no time at all, the area has turned into a battlefield.

"Hurry, get clear of the academy. Run!"

She knocks out a magical beast with one attack, then shouts at a student who's clutching his head. Although he stumbles and nearly falls, the boy breaks into a run. Behind him, a troll yanks a tree out of the ground, making ready to throw it at him.

"Walt!"

"I see it— Here we go!"

Using their superhuman leg strength, Kyle and Walt jump twice their own height. Then they slam a kick into the back of the troll's neck from either side, as if they'd rehearsed it. Before the troll can hurl the tree, they go down.

"Everyone, move quickly! This way!" Rachel is directing students who haven't made their escape yet. Jasper, Luc, and Quartz are also hard at work, ferrying away people that Aileen, Walt, and Kyle have rescued.

"Listen up: Hold the line, whatever it takes! Hey, cambion, did you finish the sky yet?!"

"Don't call me a cambion," James calls down to Isaac, erasing his wings as he lands. "I knocked down everything that was up there."

"But you didn't kill them, correct?"

"...No, I didn't. If you'd let me do that, this would go much faster." James exhales bitterly.

Auguste belts a demon that's emerged from the ground; even under the circumstances, he's smiling. "You're saying that even though you're a demon, James?"

"Look, if you're going to be like that, give back the weapon I conjured up for you."

"Huh? Not a chance! This thing is really cool. It just screams demon sword!" Even as he's talking, Auguste dodges a demon's fangs, then cleanly knocks them out with the blunt edge of his new blade. He's actually been contributing the most here.

I'd expect no less of a character who should have become a Holy Knight. No wonder Master Claude was so ready to cede the championship title to him. He's gotten used to fighting demons much too quickly!

They've gone and made him into a demon knight, though. A blade imbued with the power of the sacred sword would have killed demons, and a regular unenchanted weapon hadn't seemed effective enough, but even so... Is this going to be all right? Auguste is happy about it, but she can't help feeling that she's irrevocably warping a healthy young man's future.

"If that's a demon sword, then are these demon guns?"

"...You'd better actually be able to fix them later."

In a similar fashion, they'd imbued the sacred guns with some of James's magic energy. At this point, they're basically tranquilizer guns that won't kill demons. Walt and Kyle seem to have mixed feelings about it.

"Listen, doesn't this feel like the sort of stuff the guard unit was made for?!"

"How can you still be so laid-back at a time like this?"

"Hey, all the students are clear! Pull out!" Isaac orders. "We'll seal the gate and shut the demons inside the academy!"

Immediately, Walt catches Aileen by the waist and pulls

her to him. "Come on, sweet Ailey, we're retreating. That's enough."

"Let me go! I'm—"

"She scattered some of the purest demon snuff you can find. It's going to keep attracting demons for a month. No matter how long you fight, there'll be no end to it. We should leave before a real monster shows up."

Auguste blinks at Kyle's explanation. "Huh? Then what's going to happen to the academy?"

"A temporary closure, probably. Anyway, for now, we need to pull back. After that, you're going to explain who you are, in detail."

"That doesn't really matter—"

"How could it not matter?!" James throws his uniform jacket at her. He's standing right in front of her, and his expression is oddly intimidating. "This is an emergency, so I'm temporarily holding off on saying everything I want to say, but that's all. I have *scores* of questions!"

"He's right! I mean, are you actually Aileen Lauren d'Autriche? Because you look nothing like your portrait!"

"I can't believe something like that if you hit me with it out of nowhere, and I don't even want to in the first place! Give me proof. Understand?!"

"First, clarify whether you're a man or a woman, I'm begging you…!" Kyle pleads, and the others nod fervently. Aileen feels nothing but exasperation.

"Who I am isn't important."

"It's terribly important as far as I'm concerned."

"I'm in total agreement with Kyle! Somebody please say this is a dream!"

"Exactly! If you're a g-g-girl, that means—"

"—Wait. Something's coming."

James is staring into the distance. He's looking at the ballroom where Serena smashed the vessel of uncut demon snuff.

Come to think of it, it looked as if Serena made her escape, but...

A sudden rumble interrupts her thoughts. The earth splits, and huge claws emerge from the rift. An enormous shadow falls over Aileen and the others, growing longer.

Walt tilts his head back. He's wearing a mirthless smile. "An earth dragon... That's a monster and a half."

"A dragon?! Then..."

It can't be as strong as Claude, can it? Before she can ask, the dragon roars. The noise threatens to split her eardrums, and she instinctively covers her ears.

The dragon eagerly scans the area. Then it spots Aileen's group.

"Hurry and go! I'll distract it from the sky!" James yells.

"Walt, Kyle!"

Just as James spreads his wings, the dragon's tail sweeps through, knocking Walt and Kyle flying. Auguste runs after them, stopping its claws with his sword as it tries to attack them.

"Hey! Use the sacred sword!"

"But—"

"This one's not like the other demons! Even I might not be able to defeat—"

"James!"

The dragon swings its free arm, dashing James to the ground. Auguste is holding his own below it, determined to keep it from crushing him, but he's already on his knees.

Aileen exhales. She doesn't want to kill it. But... Picking up on her intent, the sacred sword begins to shine brighter. The earth dragon turns around. Every time it swings its tail, it knocks down buildings, and now that tail is headed her way, fast.

"Ailey! Look out—"

Before Auguste can finish his sentence, something blasts the earth dragon sideways.

Aileen blinks; she hasn't done anything yet. Auguste also looks confused. Behind him, Walt picks himself up.

"Kyle? You alive?"

"—Yeah. But what just...?"

"It looked as though an enormous mass of magic sent the dragon flying." James gulps as he crawls out of the rubble.

"What are you doing?"

The voice makes all the blood drain from Aileen's face.

Backlit by the moon, his cloak streaming in the wind, the demon king smiles. His red eyes are terribly beautiful.

"Master...Claude..."

Claude touches down lightly on a mountain of rubble. With another roar, the earth dragon charges at him.

"Master Claude! Watch ou—"

Before she can finish, she hears a light cracking noise. Claude's right arm transforms from the elbow down, growing beautiful glossy black scales and enormous claws. That arm pins the dragon with ease, then flips it over.

The earth rumbles. The dragon's eyes spin dizzily before it finally blacks out.

"......"

The demons who'd been rampaging so fiercely moments ago throw themselves to the ground, trembling. It's as if they've forgotten all about the effects of the demon snuff.

Claude swings his arm once, and it promptly returns to normal. There's no telling when it happened, but he's apparently able to transform into a demon at will now. From his expression, he might as well be standing in a gentle breeze, but his overwhelming strength makes Aileen gulp.

Th-this man… Did surviving that death flag make him completely overpowered?

The sacred sword won't work on Claude while he's human. Demons are no match for him, either. She's beginning to feel as if she may have let the most troublesome final boss live.

This is based entirely on the fact that he's gazing steadily at Aileen and only Aileen.

"What are you doing?" Claude asks again. His beautiful features are flawless. The tranquil smile on his lips is a display of the sort of relaxed confidence that is solely the privilege of the truly powerful.

An ominous wind blows. Clouds cover the night sky, rumbling with thunder, signaling that a storm is on its way.

"My darling Aileen. Shouldn't you be in the capital?"

As lightning flashes behind him, the demon king's lips slowly curve.

However, there isn't a hint of a smile in his red eyes.

"So why exactly did you take everybody and run over here?!"

"Well, I was scared! Come up with a plan, Isaac!"

"No! I told you this was all on you if he found out!"

"So even Lady Aileen is scared of something, hmm?"

"…Angry demon kings generally are scary."

In a room of the hotel that's sheltering the evacuated students,

Aileen clutches at her head. Dawn has broken, revealing a pleasant autumn sky. The refreshing weather frightens her. She can sense Claude's quiet, genuine anger in the weather. *He's mad. No, he's furious!*

To begin with, when she'd run away, he hadn't immediately come after her. That was abnormal. There's no sign that the demons are making a fuss either. Ever since the morning, when she calls to her shadow, no one answers her.

"What on earth am I supposed to do...?!"

"That's our line."

A voice that could easily be invoking a curse speaks from the corner. When she looks in that direction, James, Auguste, Walt, and Kyle are sitting at a round table, their expressions gloomy.

"A girl...the Maid of the Sacred Sword, at that...and you were running around the school festival in a duck costume."

"S-so you turned out to be somebody really important... I, um, I get the feeling I did a few things I probably, uh..."

"A woman who dressed as a man, then dressed as a woman... In other words, nothing's changed?!"

"I didn't expect Kyle to be such a blockhead, either, but the demon king's fiancée... I really didn't see that coming. Man, is a simple pay cut going to cover this one?!"

"Uh-um! I don't mind whether you're a girl or a boy, Master Ailey!" Rachel declares firmly, clenching her fists.

Aileen breaks into a smile. "Thank you, Rachel. You're the only one I can count on."

"By the way, Lady Aileen. How long are you going to stay in drag?" Luc asks.

Aileen lowers her eyes; she has her legs crossed and her chin is propped on her hand. "I thought it might lessen Master Claude's anger somewhat. Do you suppose I'd be able to get away entirely if I were a duck?"

"Miss Aileen. Brace yourself and listen." Sighing, Jasper pauses for a moment. "I went to take a look at the palace where the demon king's supposed to be...and it's frozen."

"...What?"

"From the building all the way out to the gate, it's an ice castle. From what I hear, the humans who work there are all running around town dealing with the aftermath of yesterday, and the only ones who can get in are that adviser and Beelzebuth."

Feeling hopeless, Aileen covers her face with her hands. This is no time for posturing. "I'm done for."

"...So there are times even the demon king closes his heart." There's conviction in Quartz's remark, and Aileen's shoulders slump.

"Do you suppose he hates me?"

In response to her spiritless question, Isaac and the others exchange looks. Luc gets up, encouraging her. "It's all right, Lady Aileen. The demon king is, erm, besotted with you."

"I'm not so sure. You don't think he's angry?"

"Well, no, I bet he's mad, but... Look, this isn't like you. Just be your usual confident self and get over there, the way you always do."

"But, I mean, Master Claude's never been angry with me before, so..." It's the truth, but everyone responds with awkward silence.

The only exception is Rachel. "The demon king is a kind person, isn't he? I'm sure he'll forgive you."

"H-he will, won't he? After all, he simply told me to stay in the capital and behave. I only dressed like a boy to infiltrate the academy and then disguised myself as a duck, and established a guard unit to investigate reports of demon snuff, then fought some demons. That's barely anything!"

"You seem to have fought the demon king, as well. Do you think he'll consider that barely anything?" James asks coolly. Isaac and the others quietly avert their eyes.

"She might behave better if she gets properly reamed out a couple times."

"That isn't all, is it, Lady Aileen? You were tricking him all along. Forbidding him to teleport to see you and dragging us as well as the demons into your subterfuge. I think that's probably the worst part." Luc's remark cuts like a knife.

Jasper folds his arms, sighing. "Well, yeah, that would make him mad, all right. You know he's figured it all out by now, too."

"No wonder his heart's gone as hard as ice..."

"Quartz, was that supposed to be clever?!"

"Found you, Aileen. How long are you going to keep dawdling?"

Even though they're on the hotel's fifth floor, the terrace window flies open with a bang. James and the others are over there, and when they see the demon who enters, they start to their feet in alarm. Conversely, Isaac's group looks resigned.

"Beelzebuth...and Master Keith..."

"It's been a long time, Lady Aileen. You really are dressed as a boy— And down we go."

Keith, who's arrived under Beelzebuth's arm, plants his feet lightly on the terrace. Looking sullen, Beelzebuth looses the opening shot. "Almond and the rest told us everything."

"I—I see... And, um, Master Claude...?"

"He's at the ice castle with young Denis. Building a prison."

Why? No, she can guess the reason, but she truly doesn't want to hear the answer. However, Keith shows no mercy. "He's planning to build the world's most magnificent jail so he can lock you up in it, Lady Aileen. Denis has thrown himself into drafting the blueprints!"

"Denis! He's betrayed me!"

"Well, that guy's just crazy for architecture…"

"Denis was sent to work on the reconstruction and had practically nothing to do with this affair. It isn't a question of betrayal." Beelzebuth, who's close to Denis, quickly comes to his defense.

"So… Has M-Master Claude summoned me?" Aileen's gaze is fixed on a spot on the floor, off to the side.

Keith smiles at her. "No. Milord has holed up in the ice castle. He's absorbed in his work, and in building his prison. He was smiling peacefully and saying something about how his fiancée is going to be in it soon. You take my meaning, don't you?"

"……"

"Apologize to the king before that prison is complete. You'll make it in time…probably…most likely…maybe…I'm fairly sure."

"Why won't you look me in the face, Beelzebuth?!"

"So? What will you do?"

Everyone looks at Aileen. She balls her hands into fists, then takes a deep breath. "—Bathe."

"Huh?"

"Rachel, put out a dress for me. My cosmetics, too. I'll win through seduction!"

"So it's your loss, then," Isaac says immediately, and she hurls a cushion at him.

★   ★   ★

Dress, check. Makeup, check. Claude's preferences, check.

Fully equipped, Aileen walks straight toward the palace, which is now a castle of ice. Strangely, it isn't cold. The frozen pillars and floor reflect the sun, sparkling prettily. Ice flowers bloom in the garden, and the whole scene is strangely beautiful, as if time has stopped here and only here.

Keith and Beelzebuth lead the way, a step ahead of her, and for some reason her entire group is following her. It isn't just Isaac and the others who've met Claude; James's group is there as well. Even Rachel has come along, limping on her injured leg.

For all their insistence that this is nothing to do with them, they're clearly worried about her. If she has this many companions, she'll be able to beat the demon king. Maybe.

"This way, Lady Aileen."

She's standing in front of a set of double doors so tall she has to look up to see them in their entirety. They're coated with a thin glaze of ice, and behind them is the sitting duke of Mirchetta—Claude.

She presses her lips together tightly as the doors open by themselves.

The great hall is covered in chill white mist. Aileen steps onto the thick ice of the floor. She walks very carefully, so that she won't do something as pathetic as slipping and falling.

"—I'd grown tired of waiting."

Just like a demon king greeting a hero, Claude is sitting on a chair on the dais. He's resting an elbow on a scarlet cushion embroidered with gold thread, and his beautiful face breaks into a smile. "Your timing is perfect. I was just thinking it looked lonely without its contents."

"Its contents?"

"Oh, Lady Aileen! We finished it! It's a little on the simple side, but still!"

Denis waves at her innocently from a spot near the right-hand wall. Behind him, there's a lovely cell made of ice.

It's done. As Aileen stands there, aghast, Denis runs up to her. "It's incredible, isn't it?! A prison of ice! The demon king and I made it together; I was just so excited for a chance to build something like this... I stayed up all night working on it!"

"I... I see... In other words, I'm the aforementioned contents...?"

"Go on in, please. I'm sure it will look terrific with you inside!"

"...Denis. Kid, c'mere a minute, okay?" Looking as if he's fighting a mounting headache, Jasper pulls the gleeful Denis away. She can always count on the oldest member of the group at times like this.

On the dais, Claude snaps his fingers, and the door of the prison opens. When she looks up at him wordlessly, he narrows his red eyes at her. Those eyes are telling her *Go in*.

"—I-I'm not a criminal, Master Claude."

"I know. You are my beloved fiancée."

"In that case..."

"You are important to me. It makes me spoil you in spite of myself— And this time, that was well and truly a blunder. Who would have guessed you'd disguise yourself as a boy, steal into the school, fight demons, even fight *me*... Yes, rest assured, I realized instantly why that duck had been on my mind."

Even as she shudders at the fact that he really does seem to know all, Aileen ventures a protest. "E-even you were enjoying the school festival, were you not, Master Claude...?"

"I see. So it really was you who reported me to Keith."

She's ended up pouring oil on the flames. Claude recrosses his legs. His lips curve, faintly. "It appears it's finally time to make you cry."

Aileen's cheek twitches. Slowly, Claude gets to his feet, smiling. He isn't bothering to hide his anticipation. "Now, what should I do with you? If I tore you up and crushed you with despair, what sort of face would you make? Would you beg me for forgiveness? Or would you look at me with hatred? Merely imagining it is glorious."

"I—I will categorically reject anything along those lines, as often as I must!"

"Unfortunately, I won't be able to listen to your requests. I am the demon king, after all."

"Please refrain from marching that out whenever it's convenient, if you would!"

"It's all right. Even if your mind breaks, I'll cherish you. I'll tenderly care for you myself, every day. I'll comb that lovely hair, dress you in a different gown each day, and I'll wash every inch of your skin." His lips may be smiling, but his red eyes are terrifyingly serious. Possibly because he can't quite contain his emotions, an ominous wind is blowing.

He's the demon king, through and through.

Aileen bites her lip, then takes a step forward. "—I will not apologize for what I did!" Claude's smile vanishes. He looks down at her, his face grave, but Aileen holds her head high. "I did what was correct for the woman who will become your wife."

"By deceiving me?"

"I—I do think there may have been a better way to handle that, but… Even so—I was uneasy!" Sweeping her skirts back, Aileen strides up to Claude. "You wouldn't compromise at all on going without me. You told me to sit at home quietly and behave, when we didn't know what dangers might be lying in wait here. Just what do you think I am?!"

"……"

"You're already aware that demon snuff was behind this incident. What did you intend to do if it had affected you?! Are you telling me to suffer what I went through with Master Cedric again…? And you still expect me to be quiet and wait for you?!"

Claude drops back into his chair with a thump. She hears a long, deep sigh.

"…Keith."

"What is it, milord?"

"Am I too soft?"

"We both know the answer to that already. You're crazy about her."

"Bel. What are your views?"

"Whatever your heart desires, my king. We will follow you."

"…You aside, it appears that even the other demons deceived me."

"Demon king… Can I…?"

Almond pokes his head out of Aileen's shadow. When Claude's eyes turn his way, he speaks hastily. "We worried for Aileen… Sorry for not telling you…"

"……"

"E-everyone regrets everything. Please don't abandon us..."

"A-Almond and the others only did as I told them. They aren't to blame, Master Clau—!"

Before she's finished speaking, Claude pulls her toward his chair, and she lands on his lap.

"I will decide whether they were to blame or not. I am the king here."

He's correct, of course. With some effort, Aileen swallows what she'd meant to say. Almond looks dejected.

With an arm around Aileen's waist, Claude examines Isaac and the others in the hall. "Since you followed her all this way, you must have something you wish to say to me. You may speak."

"This has been seriously exhausting. If you're the demon king, don't just try to keep her down to earth. Keep a tight grip on her, wouldja?" Isaac says.

Luc nods in agreement. "Lady Aileen isn't naturally meek and tractable, you know."

"Uh. Yeah, that's true. You really shouldn't take your eyes off her like that, Your Majesty."

"...We're no match for her. Please keep her in check as the demon king."

"Well, take it from an old guy who's got plenty of experience: You should really just smile and forgive a little thing like Miss Aileen's tendency to go off the beaten trail once in a while. That's what separates the men from the boys. Prince Cedric couldn't do it."

"Wait— Would you refrain from simply saying whatever you please?! And who has a tendency to go where now?!"

"…I see." As Aileen shouts, Claude begins to laugh, right by her ear.

"Yes, you're all correct. This was my mistake. I apologize for the trouble my fiancée has caused you."

"Just a… Master Claude! By 'trouble,' you can't possibly mean me?!"

"The demons, too. You've worked very hard. Thank you for looking after my fiancée."

"Wha—!"

They're making it sound as if Aileen has willfully caused all sorts of problems for everyone around her. However, Almond soars to Claude, looking overjoyed. "Sire! Sire, are you not mad?!"

"No. You're a good boy, Almond. Tell the others I'm not angry any longer."

"Understood!"

Claude snaps his fingers, and Almond vanishes. At the same time, the ice begins to sparkle and fall away from the great hall. It's a fantastical sight, and Aileen forgets her anger and simply watches it in awe. It's as if a wicked spell has finally come undone.

"I intend to discipline you thoroughly later, though." Claude is wearing an ill-natured smile. His whisper is oddly suggestive, and between that and what he's saying, Aileen tries to make a break for it. However, Claude keeps a tight hold on her waist.

"Now then… You seem to have collected more loyal hounds while I wasn't looking." Looking at James and the others, Claude sighs.

James takes an indignant step forward. "'Loyal hounds'? Principal, unlike you, I have no memory of being tamed by a human woman."

"I see. In other words, you're going through a rebellious phase, hmm?" Claude responds with a straight face, leaving James speechless. "You are half demon, correct? She is the woman who will be my wife. If you say I, the demon king, have been tamed, then you quite obviously come along with me as a bonus."

"A bonus."

"Don't give her too much trouble. I'll get angry—or would you prefer it if I scold you?"

Claude's red eyes glitter dangerously. Aileen, who's seeing it from a few inches away, gulps. James also seems to flinch, but then he clenches his fists and scowls. "Threaten me as much as you like. I'll never obey you!"

"What a shame. I'm sure you would be useful to me."

"Wh-where did that come from? I-it's too late for..."

"That's troublesome. I'm sure Aileen protected you for that very purpose, and yet..."

Ignoring James, whose eyes have gone wide with surprise, Aileen's face lights up. "Yes, that's it exactly, Master Claude! I'm certain he will be of great aid to you!"

"Wha... W-wait, Ailey."

"There is no talent more suitable for the era you intend to build than James."

James falls silent, as if she's caught him off guard. Claude lowers his long eyelashes. "However, demon or cambion, I wish to respect the autonomy of individuals."

"Yes, 'within the bounds you set,' correct? I understand. Leave it to me; I'll talk him around for you."

"What...did you... No, don't tell me, is that the only reason you...?" James falls to his knees.

Isaac and the others watch him with pity in their eyes, and

Auguste runs over to him. "A-are you okay, James? Well, um… It looks like you've found a job. That's great, isn't it?"

"Don't toy with me! I haven't consented to this!"

"What do you intend to do with the other four? You aren't planning to send them home for nothing."

"Of course not. That's right: Auguste, there's something I want to ask you as well."

Aileen rises from Claude's lap. Claude doesn't stop her. Sweeping her skirts out of the way, she steps lightly down from the dais, then takes Auguste's hand. That alone is enough to make him blush bright red. Aileen looks straight into his eyes. "Auguste. Would you be my knight?"

"Y-your knight?"

"I've been looking for a knight like you for a very long time. Please do come to the capital. First, I'll have you join the ranks of the Holy Knights—and you, Rachel. I'd like you to come, too."

"M-me?"

"Yes. Would you be my lady-in-waiting?" This time, she squeezes Rachel's hand. "I've wanted a lady-in-waiting who would fight alongside me and share all my secrets. It will be a career for you as well. After all, I will be empress one day."

"Oh…! Yes, I'll go!"

"Will you really?! Wonderful. And then—"

"We belong to the church!" Before Aileen can say anything further, Walt cries out and takes a step back. Apparently he's so shaken he's forgotten their existence is classified. Beside him, Kyle nods several times.

She ignores them and continues with a smile. "Then I'll just make certain *arrangements* with the church!"

"Wha— Ailey, dear, th-there's no way they'll allow that."

"It's all right. Thanks to the incident at the swordsmanship contest, we have the church by the short hairs. I'm sure they'll be willing to sell you!"

"We're getting sold to the demon king?!"

"...Umm. I don't really understand any of this, but how many more of us are there now?" Denis asks.

"Five additions," Isaac tells him tersely.

Having finished recruiting everyone, Aileen turns back to Claude, highly satisfied. "Well, Master Claude? I've proven myself useful to you, haven't I!"

"Yes. Even I am impressed by how tolerant I am," Claude says with a distant look in his eyes.

Walt cuts in, attempting to argue. "Hang on! They won't sell us; we haven't finished our assignment!"

"My, but you're stubborn. What is it?"

"Stubb— It's Serena! The business with the demon snuff! She's—"

"Under arrest," Claude tells him.

Aileen blinks. "O-on what grounds? Possession of demon snuff isn't something you can be charged with, is it?"

As far as the public is concerned, the substance doesn't even exist. That's why the church has dealt with it in secret.

Casually, Claude explains. "She tried to dose me with that demon snuff, or whatever it is. As a result, I'm punishing her with my authority as the demon king. There's nothing wrong with that."

"Sh-she gave you demon snuff?! No, don't tell me— That time at the swordsmanship contest as well?!" The development Aileen feared most has already happened. She rushes back to Claude's side, reaching out for his lovely face. Claude blinks, just once.

"W-were you all right, Master Claude? She didn't do—or cause you to do—anything immoral, did she?!"

"Immor... You know, my memories are a bit vague."

That woman! She's going to throttle her again. Slowly, Aileen's smile deepens. "I understand, Master Claude. You aren't to blame. Please don't let it concern you. I'll deal with this personally."

"......"

"Grant me permission to visit her. I'll challenge her on my own... Master Claude?"

"...I see. So you were worried about that, were you?"

Partway through, Claude's shoulders begin to shake, and then he starts laughing. Keith shrugs. "It's ill-natured of you to lie about that, milord."

"It wasn't a lie. It was retaliation for bringing up the subject of concubines."

After giving it a little thought, Aileen scowls. "You deceived me, then?"

"Not as badly as you deceived me."

He looks indifferent as he says it, and she can't really argue. Aileen grits her teeth. Claude gives her a triumphant look, then resumes his explanation. "Your demon snuff is that odd, sweet-smelling incense, isn't it? She smelled like that, so I kept my eye on her. While it doesn't affect me, it's certainly dangerous for the demons."

"...Master Claude. Will you leave the matter of Serena to me?"

Claude turns quiet eyes on her. Walt grimaces. "Ailey, we can't have that. They haven't technically sold us yet, all right?!"

"Pointless struggling aside, don't you want to complete your true mission and catch the culprit who's been spreading demon snuff around?"

"What do you mean? It isn't Serena Gilbert?"

Instead of answering Kyle's question, Aileen turns back to Claude.

The distorted things Serena had said and done when she tried to make Auguste a Holy Knight. What she must have done during the opening scenes if all had gone according to the game. There are still several things she'll need to confirm.

However, she's able to change all of that to certainty.

"Master Claude. May I have your consent?"

"For what purpose?"

"To capture Ashtart—to make you emperor."

As she makes that declaration, Aileen holds her head high. Claude looks back at her steadily.

"Very well. You are the one who will be empress after all."

No one raises an objection to the demon king's judgment.

Four months later, a proclamation was made to the effect that the Ashtart rebellion in the Mirchetta duchy was over.

Misha Academy had to be sealed off for two months, but even though an earth dragon had appeared, no one had died. The church praised Crown Prince Claude's skill in handling the matter, and the citizens of Mirchetta were deeply grateful. In addition, unstinting praise was heaped upon the students who'd held back the demon onslaught, particularly on their leader, Aileen Lauren d'Autriche, a duke's daughter and fiancée to the crown prince.

Through the incident, the crown prince demonstrated his conviction that both demons and humans were his subjects, and both fell under his guarantee of protection. While the relationship between demons and humans remained unclear, this stance proved to be a big step forward.

The troubling Ashtart had been not a demon but a human girl named Serena Gilbert. Still only seventeen, she had taken her own life. The general public found both pieces of information quite shocking. However, they were even more shocked by the announcement that one of the students who'd fought the demons was none other than a young noble of Mirchetta, a cambion whose own uncle had made frequent attempts to kill him over a period spanning many years. It proved to be a major turning point in history.

Consequently, when people passed down tales of the Ashtart incident, they spoke of it as a historic beginning. Threatened with baseless accusations of being the rebellious Ashtart, a young nobleman had gained the cooperation of the demon king, rose to meet the crisis that threatened his homeland, and had gone on to rebuild the duchy.

Snik. Snik. The sound of roses being pruned echoes through the imperial castle.

It's night in the rose garden. A girl's soft, light hair drifts in a breeze perfumed by the intense fragrance of the red blossoms. She's alone in the dim light, and as she tends the flowers under the full moon, she looks as if she's dancing. She almost seems to be plucking lives.

Just then, another shadow appears.

"Good evening, Lady Lilia."

"Oh, Lady Aileen."

Aileen has descended from an empty night sky, but although Lilia stops pruning, she doesn't seem particularly surprised. She smiles, holding an armful of red roses.

"You've returned from Mirchetta already? Cedric said things still hadn't calmed down over there."

"He's correct. However, if I have Master Claude send me this way, it only takes a moment to travel."

"Mm, that's true. And? What brings you here? Did you need something?"

"Yes. You're the one who's been tending the roses, I see. They're quite lovely."

"Yes! It's a farm you ceded to me, after all. Picking the flowers is nearly all I can do, but..."

"Opym as well?" Aileen presses her, but Lilia doesn't respond. Smiling, she clips a stem with a single flower in full bloom.

"It was careless of me not to retake this farm first chance I got."

"You were very busy, Lady Aileen. Besides, Cedric only manages the farm; it belongs to the emperor. No doubt it would have been difficult to reassert control."

"Even so— *When did it happen* for you?"

"Do I need to answer that?" Lilia holds out a rose. Its stem still has thorns. Aileen takes it.

"Serena sent you a letter, didn't she?"

That was the opening for Game 2.

"And you responded. You sent her a perfume bottle of demon snuff and filled her mind with distorted information. The fact that

Auguste becomes a Holy Knight, Walt and Kyle's hidden identities, the supposed effects of demon snuff— Did you urge her to find and slay Ashtart, as the Maid of the Sacred Sword's proxy? She did idolize you, after all. She must have scattered diluted demon snuff around the academy and searched for him with everything she had."

The potency of the incense they'd found here and there at the school had varied widely, as had its methods of use. That had probably been because Serena hadn't known how to use it, either. No doubt she'd tried all sorts of things.

"However, she just couldn't seem to find Ashtart. Growing impatient, she decided to splash demon snuff around at the school festival haphazardly, where the whole student body would be gathered. She believed the lie you'd put into her head about Auguste having the sacred sword. You were testing me, weren't you."

"Me? Test you, Lady Aileen?"

"To see whether or not I knew about the game. Whether I, like you, had memories of a past life."

The wind blows, rustling the leaves, sending petals from ailing roses drifting through the darkness. The crimson petals hide Lilia's face. However, Aileen's eyes catch the smile on her lips.

"You are Ashtart, aren't you? You assumed if I did know about the game, I was sure to go to Misha Academy, and that's why you sent that statement. Was it coincidence that you took the name Ashtart?"

"Lady Aileen, you never took a look at the fan disc, did you?"

That brief remark tells her everything she needs to know. The fact that "Ashtart" was James's demon name is a piece of background information revealed in a fan disc Aileen hasn't played.

"Heh-heh. Does that mean my knowledge of that situation outstripped yours?"

"—Even if you were able to harvest opym here, how did you manage to procure demon snuff? I can't imagine you know how to make it."

"Lady Aileen, you give your former fiancé far too little credit." Although Lilia is still smiling, she tilts her head, looking slightly troubled. "Even Cedric has a connection or two in the church."

"I see. Then Master Cedric arranged for that anonymous letter reporting that Princess Lily White's prize was demon snuff, didn't he?"

"We asked his supporters to do it. Were you surprised?"

"And the attack on the village?"

"That was the same. We simply had them scatter a little demon snuff around."

"What if someone had died? What about Serena, whom you used? You aren't going to tell me it's nothing to do with you since you didn't do anything personally, are you?"

With such a careless plan, it wouldn't have been at all strange if people had died. Aileen clenches her fists.

Lilia looks at her blankly. Then her lips curve into a smirk. "'If someone had died'?! What a laugh! Do you even hear yourself? They're just game characters!" Her peals of laughter echo in the dark sky.

"Lady Aileen, were you the type who couldn't tell games from reality in your previous life? This is a game world, you know! 'People died'? You mean characters died. Oh, but then again, you are the protagonist, aren't you?"

"This is reality! Everyone's human, just like you. If they die, they won't come back."

"Listen to me. Is there any player, anywhere, who purchases a game but won't play it because the characters will die?" Slowly letting the roses fall to her feet, Lilia places a hand over her heart. "I am the player. I took the liberty of enjoying the story in which you are the protagonist— Come, Lady Aileen. Let's play again, shall we?" She smiles, as innocently as a child. "You're the only one who can be my opponent. Everyone else is just as they were in the game. I only have to say the lines as they're written, and that does the trick. Granted, it is nice and simple. Thanks to that, I now have all my pawns."

"Are you saying that while I was occupied in Mirchetta, you romanced the characters from the first game? I don't believe that game had a harem ending."

"Goodness, that's simply a matter of juggling affection levels. It's where the player's true skill shines through." Picking up one of the roses she's dropped, Lilia continues. She sounds excited. "Oh, should we proceed to the sequel next? Or perhaps the fan disc from Game 1? This is going to be fun. It's too bad about Serena, though. If she'd also reincarnated, I thought about letting her into our circle. Well, there's no ending in the game where Serena dies by herself, so in that sense, I enjoyed it very much."

"…Unfortunately, I'm not going to play with you. I don't suppose you'd turn yourself in for this incident?"

"Have I done anything wrong? Ashtart's true identity was Serena Gilbert. You announced it yourself, Lady Aileen."

"Cedric's a louse, but he's not stupid." Isaac had said as much on an earlier occasion, and he was correct: No doubt Cedric hasn't left proof. Even if he has, he'll just say Serena did everything and cut her off, and that will be that.

A restless, rustling wind and the choking scent of roses dance between them. They're only three paces apart. Even so, the other girl looks very far away. *Even though she's reincarnated with her memories intact, like me,* she thinks.

"I'm returning Serena Gilbert to you."

Lilia's smile vanishes.

"She's alive, you see. She's been publicly declared dead, but we can revive her at any time. I'll send her to the imperial palace. I'll have her greet you formally as well—as a maidservant you personally recommended."

"A servant? What, have you turned her into a spy?"

Aileen takes a step closer. "Have I? I wonder. The girl hates me, you know."

Lilia doesn't answer, but Aileen voices her thoughts for her. "As you might imagine, she could have realized you were using her. I might have planted an idea of some sort into her head, incited her somehow... Well? What do you think? After this incident, she'll be a liability; will you kill her? But perhaps in doing so you'll be playing into my hands."

Serena knows nothing. Aileen carried out all the procedures without ever showing herself.

If she's suddenly found innocent, released, and sent to Lilia, Serena will probably assume—wrongly—that Lilia has saved her. However, Lilia will never trust her. The situation is bound to complicate itself. Instead of simply becoming a burden, Serena may even come to actively sabotage Lilia. That would be ideal.

"Besides, if she also realizes that this is a game, how do you suppose she'll see you?"

If she'd made Serena come forward as a witness, it wouldn't have accomplished much. It isn't even clear how much useful proof remains. Lilia and Cedric's involvement was indirect, and the blow wouldn't have been decisive enough to oust them. In that case, it's best to turn the girl into a bomb set on her opponent.

She takes another step. Their shadows overlap.

"Thanks to this incident, Master Claude will be rewarded by the emperor himself. He's also started to gain the trust of the human population. He's steadily advancing to the throne."

"……"

"No doubt you did enjoy yourself this time. But what of it? If you had knowledge of the game, you could have destroyed Mirchetta and kept success out of Master Claude's reach, yet all you did was play. Do you understand what I'm saying? You did nothing but muddle the game. It's made you feel as if you won, but in reality, you're losing."

Unlike the game, in real life, this won't end as a self-contained story. There is no ending.

"You can't separate reality from the game, can you?"

Aileen smiles, slowly.

"You were more formidable before you took Master Cedric. If you really want to play with me, go back and try again."

Tossing away the rose she was given, Aileen sweeps a graceful curtsy.

"Now then, if you'll excuse me, Lady Lilia. Good evening to you."

She turns on her heel. Behind her, she hears the sound of a rose being ground underfoot, but she doesn't bother looking back.

She was right after all. Wearing the uniform her employer has provided for her, Serena Gilbert smiles to herself.

In the royal palace of Imperial Ellmeyer, even the corridors are spacious and splendid. Simply walking over the velvet carpet and gazing at the paintings in the gallery makes her feel as if she's been reborn. The sparkling dress she's carrying is the very latest fashion, and she's entranced by it.

I won't have to marry that old country bumpkin. Best of all, I've actually made it to the capital!

When they'd threatened her with torture and thrown her in prison, she'd been frightened, but then they'd just as suddenly declared her innocent and released her. It must have been thanks to Lilia.

However, although she's employed at the palace, she has very mixed feelings about the fact she's a maidservant.

Lilia has explained to Serena that, since she's been declared dead, she has no rank, and so she can't make her a court lady. She's been told to "stay quiet for a while," but she finds laundry and cleaning terribly dismal.

I wonder how long she intends to make me do things like this, after I faithfully served as her proxy and everything.

"I have a favor to ask you. A cambion known as Ashtart has hidden itself at Misha Academy, disguised as a student. Please use this incense *to expose it. If you do, you will be the agent of the Maid of the Sacred Sword, and a hero—"*

That response to her letter marked the beginning of a very trying series of tasks.

To begin with, much of the information Lilia had sent her hadn't made any sense. This was particularly true when it came to the demon snuff, which was supposed to unmask the disguised demon. The letter had warned that it was dangerous to breathe too much of it, and yet the instructions on how to use it seemed almost purposefully vague. She'd only been given a small quantity, so she'd been forced to experiment. She'd crept into the academy at night and worked quite hard, burning it or strewing it around and testing its lasting effects.

When a girl with a fiancé began casting amorous glances at Auguste, she'd dropped the girl's letter in front of Professor Koenig, intending to teach her a lesson. When she realized she'd dropped a small portion of demon snuff along with it, though, she'd nearly panicked. Then the vampire incident had happened... When Koenig had gotten himself run out of the academy, she'd been extremely relieved.

However, as she'd watched Koenig get hooked on the demon snuff, she'd realized that it worked on humans, as well. That had been a lucky discovery. She'd passed it out to the male students, experimenting further. When she'd learned it also caused pleasure and worked as an aphrodisiac if diluted, she'd immediately thought *I can use this.* Regrettably, though, she hadn't received much to begin with.

It had no effect on the demon king, either.

She'd thought she might as well expose the demon where everyone could see. No doubt they'd all acknowledge her then.

Compared to that, Princess Lily White was nothing— And so she'd made her move at the school festival, but she'd had a really frightening experience there as well.

After all that effort, shouldn't Lilia have welcomed her as a friend—or even a benefactor—and had her adopted into a ducal family or something?

"...Well, it's all right."

She takes a small bottle from her pocket. She's kept back some undiluted demon snuff. There isn't much of it; less than a mouthful.

However, this is her trump card.

From the way they acted back there, it must be very unwise to possess this potion. If I tell them Lady Lilia gave it to me...

In a pinch, she should be able to blackmail Lilia.

If she treats her well, of course, Serena has no intention of doing anything of the sort. Chuckling, Serena slips the bottle into her pocket again. "What should I ask for, once things have settled down? —Oh?"

"...Serena?"

She's run into someone completely unexpected in the corridor: a young man with dark auburn hair. He looks surprised to see her, too. Serena never intended to heed the warning to "be quiet," and she strikes up a conversation with him the way she always used to do. "Auguste! What are you doing at the palace? And your clothes— Isn't that the Holy Knights' uniform?!"

The Holy Knights are the greatest of the knight brigades, under the direct control of the emperor of Ellmeyer. The deep purple cloak and the crest embellished with silver thread are formal dress only they are permitted to wear.

Auguste smiles vaguely, scratching his cheek in mild

embarrassment. "Y-yes. I took their entrance exam... They decided to let me in last week."

"That's incredible! Isn't that exam terribly difficult? You're one of the elite!"

Not only that, but its members are awarded knighthoods and high salaries to match their new station. Particularly impressive achievements are rewarded with land or further titles, as well.

"Uh... James helped me cram for the written, but I'm pretty sure I've forgotten all of it already. Ha-ha."

"Huh? The president? Don't tell me he's in the capital, too."

"...Um, yeah. Oh, but he's not the student council president anymore—"

"What are you doing, Auguste? Do you mean to be late for our audience with the emperor?"

James steps out of an intersecting corridor. He's the very picture of a young nobleman. Serena is startled, but Auguste smiles in relief. "Sorry. I'm on my way. Later, Serena."

"Wha— Wait just a minute! A cambion, in a place like this?! That can't be right!" Ordinarily they'd kill him or toss him in a dungeon. She tugs on Auguste's sleeve, but he frowns and doesn't say anything further.

Instead, James snorts. "There's nothing wrong with it. I'm Duke Mirchetta now. Prince Claude appointed me."

"Huh? You mean you're an aristocrat?" Serena's expression has stiffened.

James goes on. "Walt and Kyle are in the capital as well. They're only guards now, but I hear they'll be adopted by noble families soon."

"Adopted... Wh-why?"

"Probably because it would look a bit shabby if the guards who protected the emperor are mere commoners."

"Master Auguste, Master James. Prince Claude is calling for you."

She recognizes that voice as well, and she growls the name. "Rachel Danis…"

Rachel is there, dressed in a fine black uniform. It's the livery of the d'Autriche ducal family, who are highly respected in this palace. Serena, who's been dumped into the same place as a serving maid, has choked down her irritation and bowed to people in those uniforms many, many times, so she's intimately familiar with them.

Why?! The house of d'Autriche?! However did she get in…?!

"He says he would like you to attend the imperial audience. I'll show you the way. Come with me."

"All right. Let's go, Auguste."

As the three of them start to walk away, Serena runs after them. "Stop right there! What on earth is this? How can all the members of the student council be in the capital?!"

Not only that, but every one of them outranks Serena. Granted, Serena's bound to be treated in a similar fashion later on, but even so.

"Something is very wrong here! What happened?! Explain all this!"

Even though Serena's talking to them, none of the others answer. Before long, the corridor takes them to the door of a parlor used by the imperial family. When the guard bows to the trio, she sees red. This guard once threw dirty laundry at her and told her to take care of it.

"Excuse me!"

"Leave."

As she tries to catch the hem of Auguste's jacket one more time, a cold voice cuts in. It's Rachel. She's standing in front of the door, barring her way. Serena stares at her in disbelief.

"His Highness the crown prince and Lady Aileen, his fiancée, are in this room. Refrain from causing a disturbance."

"Wha— Wh-why do I have to hear this from you?! Just who do you think you are?!"

"I am Lady Aileen Lauren d'Autriche's lady-in-waiting."

In other words, when Aileen Lauren d'Autriche becomes empress, Rachel will have the authority equivalent to the chief lady-in-waiting. She's asserting that, as things stand, she's fully qualified to give Serena orders.

"You are just a servant. You can't enter this room without permission. Leave."

"What's the matter? It's quite lively out there, Rachel."

The doors open from the inside, and a cool voice reaches them. Walt has opened one half of the double door, while Kyle opens the other. They aren't wearing school uniforms, either. They're in military dress with beautiful gold braids, the sort the demon king's adviser had worn on an earlier occasion.

Then a young noblewoman emerges from the room, and everyone bows to her. Serena gulps.

It's Princess Lily White. The one who trounced her.

Immediately, a variety of connections form in her mind. Ailey Calois, who was actually a girl. If that had been Princess Lily White, then, in other words—

"And who might you be?" Aileen Lauren d'Autriche says with an elegant smile.

They'd seen each other at the school festival. There's no way she doesn't remember Serena. In asking who she is, she's clearly mocking her. Serena clenches her trembling fists.

It's all a farce. There's no way anything so ridiculous could be allowed. "What on earth is this?! This utter—!"

As she starts to tear into her, someone points a sword at the base of her throat.

"Leave."

It's Auguste. His voice is so cold she can't believe it, and for a moment, she stops breathing.

They'd been together on the student council. She'd brought him snacks and looked out for him on more than a few occasions. She'd been such a good friend to him. And now this is the treatment she gets? James doesn't say anything, either. He's a demon; why is he acting like he's above her? Kyle and Walt don't even glance her way.

"Auguste, don't frighten the poor thing. So you're all here, then. Master Claude, it's time to depart for the audience chamber."

"Yes."

"Master Claude…!"

The beautiful demon king has appeared from the depths of the room. Serena turns beseeching eyes on him. He's her last hope. She'd taken good care of him; he must remember her! There might still be some lingering effect from the potion as well. "It's me, Serena Gilbert! I assisted you at Misha Academy… Um, what is all this?! That woman can't possibly be your fiancée. After all, you were kind to me! Remember, Master Claude?!"

"Serena Gilbert is dead."

His flat response sends a sudden chill shooting through her.

The house of Gilbert held an impoverished rural title, and she hadn't regretted losing it. Cutting her ties to them and having

Lilia give her an appointment had seemed like a much better option. Even when they'd falsely accused her of being Ashtart, it had seemed like a fine way to retaliate against her family; she hadn't been able to stop laughing about it.

But what if Lilia doesn't appoint her to any position? When she'd told her to "be quiet for a while," hadn't there been distaste lurking behind her smile?

She touches the pocket that has the little bottle in it. Rather than a trump card, this might actually be her only reliable lifeline.

Have I made a grave mistake?

She looks at the people who were her fellow students a few short months ago. If they are accompanying the crown prince to an imperial audience, when Claude eventually becomes emperor, this group will probably be his inner circle.

And as things stand, Serena's only a maid.

While she stands there silently, Aileen Lauren d'Autriche passes in front of her. Impulsively, she tries to strike her, but Walt blocks the attempt.

Even so, she can't help herself. Her anger and unease won't be silenced.

"You! You set me up, didn't you! Even though you're a shameless hussy who switched from Master Cedric to Master Claude…! Master Claude, she's deceiving you! You'll never find happiness with a woman like thi—"

The demon king looks at her. Then, with eyes that seemingly contain no emotion whatsoever, he snaps his fingers.

Immediately afterward, in a trivial accident that was nonetheless a total disaster for the victim, a lone maidservant fell into the palace cesspit.

*   *   *

Aileen fully intended to give as good as she got, and when Serena disappears, she blinks. Then she glances carefully up at Claude.

"Where did you send her? Surely not to— Not again..."

"I don't know what you're talking about."

His expression is cool, and she sighs. However, Rachel promptly cautions her. "Lady Aileen, the appointment for the audience..."

"I know. Rachel, after the audience, could you make sure there's tea waiting for us in the castle in the forest?"

"Yes, of course."

As a lady-in-waiting, Rachel has far surpassed her expectations. Her etiquette had always been flawless. The d'Autriche housekeeper, who had also served as the chief lady-in-waiting at the palace, dotes on her.

Even though he'd nearly ended up in tears, Auguste had passed the entrance exam for the Holy Knights. This meant they now had a man in an organization where they'd previously had no eyes or connections. He'd also gotten in before Marcus, who is a member of Lilia's camp. That will probably prove to be a major accomplishment down the line.

The fact that Walt and Kyle have been taken in as Claude's guards is also important. The church isn't a monolith; some of its members side with Cedric. The fact that they've extracted two of their outstanding Nameless Priests is bound to be useful down the road.

James has been appointed duke. Claude is responsible for that particular coup. He'd collected proof of the corruption in the house of Mirchetta, and had virtually taken over the duchy. Then he'd pressured them to accept James as the duke, after revealing the fact that James was half demon, and publishing his uncle's misdeeds.

At that point, James had begun calling him Prince Claude instead of demon king. Apparently he's resigned himself to the reality of the situation.

Someday, he'll be the first person to build a territory where demons and humans live side by side. The fact that the territory will be the Maid of the Sacred Sword's birthplace has great political significance as well.

That said, Duke Mirchetta is still alive, so for now, James is studying politics in the capital under Prime Minister d'Autriche. By his own request, he's living in the former abandoned castle alongside the demons. Beelzebuth has started becoming weirdly competitive with him around, while Keith is putting on airs since he's been at the job longer, but they seem to be getting along passably well.

The entire group is about to receive an audience with the emperor. This is tantamount to a public declaration that they will be Claude's closest advisers one day.

Cedric and Lilia are also solidifying their camp. Lilia in particular has pulled off the feat of conquering all the love interests from Game 1. Aileen's group needs to pull together talent that can compete in every field.

"Are you sure it's all right to continue treating Isaac and the others as usual, without granting them an audience with the emperor?" Claude asks on their way to the audience chamber. Aileen nods.

"Yes, they say that's best. Keeping things this way will be a great help for me as well. It would be dangerous to have all our allies in the palace, and Jasper says he likes exposing the sins of the palace denizens."

"They do seem to enjoy working at the Oberon Trading Firm more than here."

"Well, they've finally made it back from Mirchetta. There's a lot of work to do."

"True… By the way. Aileen. All we've been doing is working, and I still haven't gotten around to disciplining you yet."

He's made this pointed remark several times already. Aileen evades it with a smile. "Let's think about that once we're safely through the audience, shall we?"

"You're putting me off more and more with each passing day…"

"Save the lovers' spat for later, demon king and sweet Ailey," Walt murmurs playfully from right beside them.

Kyle grimaces. "Not Ailey, Walt. It's Lady Aileen."

"I just can't seem to shake the habit. Don't be so uptight. Right, Auguste?"

"I-I'm doing my best to correct it! Besides, Ailey's a girl— Oops."

Auguste has slipped up right after saying he wouldn't, and Aileen smiles at him. "If you'll stick to using it in private, I don't mind if you call me Ailey, Auguste."

"Hearing you talk like Ailey when you're in a dress is kind of a letdown…"

"Really? I think it's charming," Claude says, straight-faced.

Only James retorts, calmly. "Prince Claude. Do that sort of thing to your heart's content later. You're free to discipline her or do whatever you like."

"That's true, but I already have something to think about after the audience."

"Oh, do you? What might that be?"

They're approaching the audience chamber where the emperor is waiting, but Claude is still the same as always. *Even though I'm so nervous that I feel sick to my stomach...!* This will be her first imperial audience as Claude's fiancée. She was Cedric's fiancée once, and now she's standing beside his half brother. How will that look to the emperor?

However, Claude blows away Aileen's tension with a single remark.

"I've been thinking that it's about time we kissed."

Correction—he destroys the atmosphere entirely.

"Once I introduce you to the emperor, you will have been formally acknowledged by my father. What do you say?"

"Wha...? What...? What do I—?!"

"I could give you a disciplinary kind of kiss as your first, if you'd prefer. What sort would you like?"

"Please just stop talking, Master Claude! I'll hear you out later!"

He's publicly revealed how far their relationship has progressed, and Aileen practically shrieks. The others carefully avert their eyes, and while she's grateful for their kindness, it's still painfully awkward.

"I think it's important. You're saying it's all right if I choose, though? I see..."

"I am not saying that! For now, don't damage the mood any more than you have already! I am about to have my first audience with the emperor as your fiancée, Master Claude! Whatever will he think of me?"

"Never mind that. You don't have to look at anyone but me, Aileen."

He says her name sweetly, and she feels something soft press against her forehead.

There's a moment's pause, and then she leaps backward. She puts a hand to her forehead, flushing bright red. He's kissed her there.

"A-a-as I *just* told you, not here, not in public...!"

"Well, you kept putting me off— It will be all right. You suit me quite well."

This man really doesn't fight fair.

Using her chagrin as a springboard, Aileen faces forward, throwing her shoulders back.

"Of course I do."

"Then shall we go, Aileen?"

Go, with their new companions, straight down the road to the imperial throne.

Afterword

It's a pleasure to meet you, or perhaps it's good to see you again. My name is Sarasa Nagase.

Thank you very much for picking up my humble attempt at a novel. This is a sequel about Aileen, the demon king, and their merry friends.

This edition is almost forty pages longer than its online version. When they told me I'd be able to add to the book, I wavered between fleshing out multiple scenes or putting in a whole new episode, and ultimately decided to go with the latter.

I hope both those who've previously read the online novel and those who haven't will enjoy the demon king's additional appearance, even though he might seem a little off in it.

I have one more piece of good news: Gekkan Comp-Ace has decided to serialize a manga version of *I'm the Villainess, So I'm Taming the Final Boss*! Even now, as I'm telling you about it, it feels like a dream. The artist will be Anko Yuzu. I've seen the roughs and the storyboards already, and they're truly magnificent. You'll be able to find more details on the official site as they're released, so when the series starts, please do take a look at it!

And now for the thank-yous.

To Mai Murasaki: Thank you so much for drawing these beautiful illustrations, even though you were so busy. I feel blessed every time I look at them.

To my supervising editor: I'm in your debt for a great many, many things. Please continue to look out for me.

I'd also like to thank the proofreaders, the members of the editorial department, the designers and marketing personnel, and all the people who were involved in the making of this book. I'm deeply grateful to all of you.

Finally, to everyone who picked up this book: Thank you very much for sticking with me this far. Not only has this story been published as a physical novel, but it's getting a manga adaptation as well, and it's all thanks to you. Please honor me with your continued support.

Now then, with prayers that we'll meet again...

Sarasa Nagase